Midsummer, Marriage, and Murder

Also by A. L. Jensen

Hygge and Homicide
Midsummer, Marriage, and Murder
Murder by Nordic Design

COMING SOON:
Death By Glögg
Forest Bathing and Mindful Murder

BY LIISA KOVALA
Like Water for Weary Souls
Sisu's Winter War
Surviving Stutthof

A HYGGE HOUSE
COZY MYSTERY

Midsummer, Marriage, and MURDER

A. L. JENSEN

ISBN: 978-0-9950834-5-5 (paperback)

ISBN: 978-0-9950834-6-2 (ebook)

Cover Design: Deranged Doctor Design

Author Photo: Mia Jensen

Published by: House of Karhu

www.houseofkarhu.com

First edition: 2026

To Carita
for Santa Lucia and Star Boys

Nordic Words & Concepts

- Aurora Borealis: Northern lights visible from northern regions like Sweden, Denmark, Finland, & Canada

- Hygge: A quality of coziness and contentment (Denmark & Norway)

- Kippis: Version of the toast "cheers" (Finland)

- Korvapuusti: Translates to "slapped ears," the shape of a cinnamon bun (Finland)

- Kulta: Translates to "gold," a term of endearment like darling or sweetheart (Finland)

- Midsommarkrans: Wreath made of flowers and leaves worn as a crown during Midsummer (Sweden)

- Mummu: Grandmother (Finland)

- Pulla: A braided coffee bread with cardamom (Finland)

- Riisipiirakka: A rice pie with a rye crust (Finland)

- Ruisleipä: A dark sourdough rye bread (Finland)

- Sisu: The concept of courage, determination, and bravery

in the face of adversity (Finland)

- Stuga: Cozy cabin or cottage (Sweden)

- Taiga: Boreal forest (Canada, Russia, Nordic countries)

Chapter 1

Sunlight streamed in through the paned glass window, illuminating the bride-to-be in her flowing white gown, a vision of beauty and serenity. The dress was in its final stages of construction, but already I could tell it was ideal for Grace Bradshaw's upcoming nuptials. Grace was on edge, and the tension was palpable in the backroom of Annabelle's Stitchery, where Annabelle had set up a corner especially for fittings.

Christie and I waited with bated breath. Grace smiled at us before turning around on the raised platform to examine her reflection, her expression open and expectant, and her hands fluttering at the gauzy fabric at her sides.

She caught one glimpse of herself and covered her mouth with her hands, her eyes wide. "Oh no! I can't believe it. What are we going to do?" Tears formed in her eyes as she stared at herself in the three-way full-length mirror.

I bit my tongue and glanced at Christie, who sat across from me on a vintage couch upholstered in red velvet, her legs and arms crossed tightly. It seemed she wanted to say something too, but she restrained herself. I held a pillow on my lap, playing with the tassels to hide my nervousness.

The wedding was two weeks away, and despite Christie's organization, problems—and Christie's stress level—were mounting.

And I had my own problems to worry about. Hygge House's first floor renovations had gone well, but we weren't ready for overnight guests upstairs. Time was ticking. And now the bride was unlikely to say yes to the dress.

Annabelle fussed with the bodice of Grace's gown, pinning it where it was too loose and marking it where it needed to be let out. After a few minutes, she placed her hands on the bride-to-be's shoulders.

"Don't worry. We need to make a few adjustments. This is exactly why I do this fitting, to make sure your gown fits you well on the day." She gave Grace a reassuring smile. I imagined her frustration at having to fit in the alterations at the last minute, but she did not reveal that it was a problem. Thank goodness for Annabelle.

Grace's shoulders relaxed, and her expression softened. "I mean, I love it so much, but it doesn't fit right. Will it be ready on time?"

Annabelle squeezed her hand and nodded. "Of course. I guarantee it." I recognized her motherly tone from the time I'd visited her about Hygge House's curtains before our opening.

"It's a good thing we got you here for the fitting then, isn't it?" Christie asked. She sounded only mildly irritated, but she'd had difficulty getting Grace to Annabelle's for the fitting in the first place, along with other issues, like finalizing the guest list.

I shot Christie a look, and she shrugged. It was not a good time to further upset the bride.

"Well, I think you look drop-dead gorgeous," I said, noting the distressed look on Grace's face. "Annabelle will work wonders with your dress. Everything is going to be perfect."

I caught myself saying the words, knowing full well I shouldn't promise anything as grandiose as perfection, but it was too late. Excellence was the goal, of course, but after what had happened at Hygge House earlier this spring, I didn't want to tempt fate.

Grace put her hands on her hips, surveying herself in the mirror, and turning from side to side to see every angle. It was, in fact, a spectacular design. The gauzy fabric flowed to the floor, with delicate flowers floating from the bodice to the skirt and gathering on the train, and tiny fabric-covered buttons down the back. I could imagine Grace in the garden at Hygge House, saying her vows underneath a wedding arch interlaced with vines and flowers. Annabelle had outdone herself.

"I almost forgot something. Give me a sec." Annabelle bounced out of the room and returned with a long veil and a flower crown. Oh, to have Annabelle's youth and energy. My middle-aged body didn't feel so bouncy anymore. At least, not in that way.

"Is it too much?" Grace asked, touching the fine fabric adorned with embroidered flowers. "The veil is gorgeous, but I'm not sure about the floral crown—"

"You said you wanted a midsummer theme, and a mid-sommarkrans is traditional." Christie reminded Grace of the planning discussions we'd had in the last several weeks. She'd suggested the floral crown, reminiscent of midsummer cele-brations in Sweden and other Nordic countries. "Try it on at least. If you don't like it, you don't have to wear it."

Annabelle placed the veil on Grace's head and secured it with pins, then held the flower crown over her head, lowering it slowly as if she were a fairy queen. Grace turned back toward the mirror, a smile spreading across her face. "Oh, it's so lovely."

Christie and I applauded. Grace's vision of a midsummer wedding had been in the works for months, but seeing her bedecked in her gown and crown was like a magical fairy-tale moment, with Annabelle as the fairy godmother transforming her into a princess. Were Christie and I the evil stepsisters, trying to get Grace on schedule? Probably, but if it meant the wedding would go off without a hitch, we'd have to deal with it.

Grace's smile vanished, and tears slid down her cheeks. She sniffled.

I found a tissue in my purse and stood up to pass it to her. "Are you okay?" I asked. Were those happy tears, or was something else happening?

Grace wiped her tears and blew her nose, nodding as she cried. "Yeah, I guess. It's all like a dream. I'm just ..."

"What, Grace? Are you nervous about the wedding?" Something was going on with her, and I couldn't read her expression.

Annabelle stood back, concern written on her face. "If it's the dress, I can change anything you don't like, and I promise adjustments will be a breeze. Nip it in here and let it out there. Nothing to worry about." After the hours she had put into consulting, designing, and sewing the gown, I couldn't help but feel for her. Grace was no Bridezilla, but she wasn't as engaged with the wedding preparations as we'd expected. No pun intended.

"Goodness, no. The gown is gorgeous." Grace shook her head. "I've been emotional lately. I'm excited about the wedding, but as it gets closer, there are so many issues to deal with. And I miss him, you know?"

I took Grace's hand and nodded, unsure of what to say. "That makes sense. You have every reason to feel mixed emotions. But your brother will be with you in spirit."

I didn't know how to comfort her. She'd lost her brother, Owen, only two months earlier, on the morning of Hygge House's official opening. I'd been the one to find his body sprawled out on the floor of our breakfast nook.

Despite the capture of Owen's murderer, Grace's excitement about the wedding did not diminish her grief for her brother.

"We're here for you. Tell us what you need," I added.

"Thanks, Minna. I can count on you. And Christie. All of you. I'll be okay." She plastered on a bright smile, turned away from the mirror, and stepped off the raised platform. "I guess jitters are normal, right?"

I nodded, and Christie agreed. Annabelle took off Grace's crown and veil before picking up the train. With caution, they padded to the change room.

"What's wrong with Grace?" I glanced toward the room where they had disappeared, keeping my voice low. "She doesn't seem like herself lately."

"I know what you mean, but I get it. Owen hasn't been gone very long, and a wedding is a big deal. She's probably going through a lot right now." Christie pulled out her clipboard from her oversized purse. "I have so many questions, but it's not the right time."

A few minutes later, Grace emerged from the change room, wearing a pale-yellow summery dress ideal for the warmth of the day. Her eyes were dry now, and she'd applied some colour to her cheeks and lips, giving her a fresh look, as though she hadn't been crying.

Before leaving Annabelle's Stitchery, we arranged a date and time for the last fitting, ensuring Grace had it scheduled in her calendar app. We thanked Annabelle and followed Grace out onto Heritage Street. The late-morning sun was already warm and promised a beautiful afternoon.

"Do you have time for a coffee?" Christie asked. "We should talk about the final wedding details and the guest list." She nodded toward Boreal Beanery across the street. She sounded cautious, not wanting to press Grace. But she was right to ask. Our to-do list was too long.

"Oh, I'm so sorry. I have a hair appointment in a few minutes." She touched her purple streaked hair. "And then I'm meeting Jack for lunch, but I promise to get his guest list today. There's been some back and forth with family members, but it should be sorted out now." Grace frowned, and a line deepened on her forehead. "My list is so short, it's barely a list. No family. A few friends." She forced a laugh. "Thank goodness Eloise is coming from Paris to be my maid of honour."

"Yes, it's lovely to have your best friend at your side. Right, we'll be in touch soon. In the meantime, I'm working on getting those guest rooms ready for his family." I touched Grace's arm. "You may not have a lot of family coming, but you've got us."

Grace threw her arms around me, stifling a sob. "I appreciate that." She released her grip and turned away.

Christie and I crossed the street, heading toward Boreal Beanery without having to ask one another if we needed coffee. Of course, we did.

"You think she's okay?" Christie asked, stepping onto the curb and turning toward the shop.

"Who knows? But we should keep an eye on her. She's not telling us everything. In the meantime, let's do everything we can to make her fairy-tale wedding magical."

I followed Christie inside; the aroma of freshly brewed coffee enticed me. Grace wasn't the first bride to have nerves before the wedding, and she certainly wouldn't be the last. Christie and I needed to get her down the aisle with no major catastrophes.

Chapter 2

The next day, we gathered around the table under the covered verandah for our regular Sunday brunch and Elsi's famous Finnish pancakes. They were Sofia's favourites, especially served with fresh blueberries and cream.

Hugo Dogberg lounged in a sunspot at the top of the stairs, eyeing the yard for something to chase: a squirrel or chipmunk, even a butterfly or hummingbird, while Freya and Astrid lay sprawled out together nearby.

"Well, ladies. What do you have planned for today?" Mom asked, pouring me another cup of coffee in my favourite mug. She offered Sofia more coffee, too, but she declined.

"One cup is enough for me, Mummu." Sofia smiled. My daughter's love of coffee had not yet reached my own. She was young. There was time. It was probably better if she didn't drink too much coffee. For some Finns, coffee was like drinking water. If an intravenous drip for coffee existed, I'm pretty sure many Finns would hook up. Including myself.

I added some cream and sat back in my rattan chair, gazing out at the garden my mother had been patiently tending, encouraging the flowers to blossom in time for the upcoming nuptials. "Garden looks great, Mom."

"Thanks, darling. It's coming along nicely. If we trim back some of those bushes at the far end, we'll get more light in that part of the garden." Mom had learned every trick in the book, including the right fertilizers, plant food, and just the right amount of water. Luckily, nature was providing the sunshine we needed. I just prayed the pleasant weather would last for the rehearsal dinner and wedding.

Sofia brushed crumbs from her croissant off her skirt. "I'll ask Tyler to help you with that, Mummu."

"Oh, good idea," Mom said. "He's becoming quite a horticulturist, your Tyler."

Sofia grinned. "Well, he's learning from the best."

"I'm popping into Henri's Hardware to check on the wedding arch." I sprinkled a little sugar and cinnamon onto a pancake, rolled it, and popped it into my mouth. Delicious. "Want to come?"

Mom sat straighter and gave me a quizzical look. "Whatever for? I need nothing from the hardware store." She sounded a little defensive.

Her response surprised me, but I shrugged it off. "Just thought you'd like to see the bridal arch."

"And Henri is there," Sofia added with a twinkle in her eye. "Don't you want to say hello?"

"Hush now." Mom swatted Sofia with a napkin. "It makes no difference to me whether he's there."

Did Sofia know something about my mother and Henri that I didn't? I'd have to ask her later, but I was already running late. "Come on, boy." I said to Hugo. "Let's go."

Hugo jumped up and bounded toward me, his tail wagging. My mother slipped him a piece of bacon. Hugo's devotion was unwavering, especially when his reward was treats and lots of ear rubs.

"See you later. If James comes by, tell him to meet me at Henri's. With his truck."

Mom and Sofia waved as I left, and I marvelled at how close my mother and daughter had become in the past few months. It had been more difficult when Sofia and I lived in Toronto with her father, Peter. It wasn't that far, but careers and school kept us from Lakewood, and Mom rarely visited the big city. Too loud. Too busy. Too much traffic. Lakewood suited her better. She had a point. Apparently, it suited me better, too. It had just taken me a few decades to figure that out small-town living was more my speed.

Hugo and I trotted towards the garden shed, freshly painted with the iconic red of Scandinavian cottages and with garden boxes in front of the small windows overflowing with ivy and flowering plants. Tuuli, my trusty mint green 1950s Schwinn bicycle, already had her trailer hooked up to the back, and Hugo dutifully jumped in. After months of living in Lakewood, Hugo understood the drill. Tuuli never failed to bring us somewhere interesting in town, and there were often doggie treats to enjoy.

In fact, Hugo had become quite popular in Lakewood. Sofia regularly posted his images on social media feeds, and viewers lapped them up. And he was well loved by the local business owners, welcomed wherever we went. He was becoming something of a celebrity. I just hoped it wasn't going to his head.

Cycling on the boardwalk along Long Lake was my favourite way to travel from Hygge House, a few kilometres from the centre of town, to Heritage Street. On a morning like this, it was easy to forget the wedding to-do list for Hygge House. Instead, I relished the warmth of the sun on my skin and focussed on the green vista ahead of me.

The lake was a serene cerulean blue, like a picture postcard, and the sky, well, it was sky blue in the best way possible. Light clouds wafted overhead, and sparrows chirped in the trees overhanging the boardwalk, making for an enchanting journey. It was hard not to have one's spirits lifted on a day like today.

Hugo and I passed a group of seniors on their daily stroll, and a couple jogged in the opposite direction. Everyone nodded, or smiled, or said hello. It had taken a few months, but now I was used to all the smiling and nodding as I pedaled. Unlike Toronto, where I'd lived for decades before moving back to Lakewood, the whole town seemed to be acquainted with one another. In Toronto, I avoided eye contact and small talk with strangers. Only during tourist season did Lakewood sometimes feel a little like walking through a strange neighbourhood in the city, with curious onlookers gawking at every flower, duck, and tree.

I turned off the boardwalk and headed up Heritage Street. My mother Elsi's shop, Nordic Cozy, a staple for decades in town, was closed as it always was on Sundays, giving all three of us a day off to enjoy as we pleased. Since Sofia had moved to town in early spring, I didn't spend as much time at the store. A few hours a week at most.

As I passed Boreal Beanery, I glanced through the window to see if Sarah or her husband Brian Bean were there, but the lineup at the counter suggested they would be too busy to see me going past. Next door, the scent of flowers from Winterberry and Willow Floral Shop floated in my direction, reminding me to check with Lucy Chen on Grace's bouquets and the head-table centrepiece.

I crossed over toward Henri's Hardware on the corner of Heritage and Pine Street, pulling Tuuli onto the sidewalk beside the store, glancing at the crooked sign as I always did. Part of me wanted to mention that he should get it fixed. But the other part would miss that eccentric detail.

Tuuli would be safe on the sidewalk. Since Owen Bradshaw's murder a few months earlier, I'd been less relaxed about safety. When I first moved back to Lakewood, I couldn't imagine anything untoward happening in our small town. Until I found his body on our doorstep, that is. Lakewood was quaint, but the unexpected could happen. I'd learned that all too well recently.

I glanced at the small parking area, noticing a familiar truck. James must be lurking around the store today. Not that I was *eager* to see him, but he hadn't made it to his open invitation for Sunday brunch, and I was a little disappointed. Was it because he hadn't brought a box of cinnamon rolls from Fika and Frosting? Maybe.

But I enjoyed seeing his handsome face at least as much as a freshly baked cinnamon roll.

With Hugo on the leash, I pushed open the heavy door to Henri's Hardware; the bell above chirped to signify my arrival. For a Sunday, the store was pretty busy. It had been a few weeks since I'd last been there, and I wasn't expecting the crowd. We were on the heels of spring, so I should have expected the shoppers getting their yards and gardens ready.

I searched around for Henri or James, jostling past customers with full baskets, and guiding Hugo away from the shelves with all their unfamiliar scents that drew his immediate and undivided attention. We paused briefly to let Hugo get a pet from a young boy. He spoke to Hugo in a gentle voice and they became immediate friends. If only it were that easy for adults to connect. Thank goodness for the ones we've had since childhood.

"Hallo, Minna," Henri called from the back of the store, giving me a wave across the aisle. "Meet me at the garden centre. I'll be right out."

I waved back and made my way past the shelves toward the back of the store and through the rear entrance, open now to the temporary garden centre that took up half the parking lot. Besides potted plants and hanging baskets, the garden centre had bird feeders, outdoor furniture, string lights, and wind chimes. The garden centre reminded me summer was around the corner. But then, too, was Grace and Jack's wedding.

I picked up a wind chime with a fairy holding a flower and held it up, listening to its dulcet tones, determined to find somewhere to place it, in the garden or perhaps in the woods behind the house. I loved finding treasures and unexpected things, like fairy doors at the base of trees, and wanted Hygge House to be surrounded by brief moments of unexpected pleasure.

"Looks beautiful out here, Henri," I said, admiring the festive atmosphere.

"Indeed. Summer's nearly here and we're ready for it." Henri plopped a large pot onto a wheelbarrow and pushed it towards the makeshift counter and cash register. For an older guy, he was very fit. After his heart attack scare a few years ago, James had created an exercise routine for his father. Perhaps he could do the same for me.

"James, ring this up for Sally and carry it to her car, will you?" From behind the register, James popped up and nodded at his father before winking at me.

"Ah, Henri's enlisted you to work today. I didn't take you for the gardening type." I crossed my arms and smiled at my friend.

"I'm a man of many talents." James grinned. "Actually, I'm only here until Tyler shows up to replace me." He checked his phone. "Any minute now. Not like him to be running late."

"That's why you didn't make it to brunch?" I asked. It was unusual for James to pass up Elsi's pancakes.

"Yeah, I meant to text you with my apologies. Couldn't keep my old man in the lurch."

Sally Murphy strolled up with hanging baskets in each hand. She placed the baskets on the long table near the cash register, then greeted me in her lovely Irish accent.

"How are you, dear one?" she asked. "I imagine Elsi doesn't need pre-made baskets. I wish I had her green thumb. We just couldn't wait until the Horticultural Society's garden party, but I'll get the rest of my plants there." Sally blushed.

"I get it," I replied. "I have difficulty keeping any plants alive, but Mom loves it so much. Good thing, too. Grace's wedding is taking place in the garden, as long as the weather holds."

"Oh dear," Sally replied. "What if it rains? Or snows?" Her eyebrows squinted, and I could tell she was thinking of all the other disasters that could affect the special day. I loved Sally, but she leaned toward catastrophe.

"You know Christie. She always has a Plan B. If the weather doesn't cooperate, we'll hold the ceremony in Taiga Hall. We have plenty of space." I hoped Sally would hear my confidence, but the truth was, an outdoor wedding was risky. For weeks now, I'd kept my fingers and toes crossed.

Sally looked visibly relieved. "Smart girls, you and Christie. I'm looking forward to it. Sean and I can't stop talking about our lovely anniversary party. Delightful. And we haven't had a wedding around here in ages, it seems." She glanced from me to James and back to me again. "Of course, we may have a few more in our future."

Heat rose in my cheeks, but I smiled politely. "Lovely to see you, Sally. Best to Sean."

"Here we go, Sally. Let's bring this to your car," James suggested.

I mouthed 'thank you' to him and watched as they strode away, chatting about something or other. Sally may be one of my mother's oldest friends, but she could talk your ear off if you let her. I imagined Sally was the source of much of my mother's town gossip, but I supposed Christie and I would be like them in a few years, whispering over our tea and feigning shock.

With James and Sally headed to the other side of the parking lot, I turned to look for Henri, but he had vanished. My fairy wind chime crashed against my legs as I searched. For an older gentleman, he sure was quick on his feet.

I popped back into the store, where I found Henri chatting to a big man in a plaid shirt and a baseball cap. The man had his back to me. Beside him, a petite woman spoke with her hands waving. Henri was clearly dealing with something. I stepped back into the garden centre.

A few moments later, he returned from the bowels of the store, struggling with a large shrouded object. As if on cue, Tyler arrived and rushed over to help him carry the massive structure.

"Ah, thanks, young Tyler. Just in time. Might've had myself another heart attack." Henri laughed, and Tyler took over, moving

it so I could have a good look out of the way of the other customers.

"Sorry about that. Reggie's having some critter problems,
it seems. That's what happens when you live in a shack in the
woods. But 'tis the season," he said, chuckling.

"Reggie White? The guitar player? Northern Spirit is playing
at the wedding." I'd seen the band decades earlier. Amazing that
they were still going strong.

Henri raised his shoulders. "Far's I know, Reggie only plays
occasionally these days. He replaces the regular guy, Jed, from
time to time."

"Jed's the one with all the kids?" I asked, trying to remember
everyone's names. Floyd had given me a list of who was coming,
but I couldn't keep them all straight. Except for Norah, the lead
singer and the only female in the band.

"Yup, that's him. Wife doesn't like his going out to so many
gigs anymore. Did you know he's my accountant?" Henri chuckled. "Never know with these musician types."

"I have some mice in the garden shed. And I'm worried about
what's in the attic. I've been hearing some strange noises up there.
Can you give me some of that stuff?"

"Will do. Don't need mice upsetting the wedding guests.
Okay, ready to see it? One, two, three ..." Henri swooped off the
dust cover for the big reveal.

"Oh my goodness, Henri. It's so beautiful. I was expecting
something really simple, but this is so special." I moved closer
to inspect the fine woodwork—the swirls carved into the wood,
flowers, and vines intertwining. "You're so talented."

Henri looked chuffed. "I don't get opportunities to do this
kind of work very often. It was a great pleasure," he said. "Anything
to make Grace's wedding special. The poor girl has had a tough
go of it. First, her parents died in that terrible car accident. Then
her brother ..." Henri shook his head and held back tears. What a
kind soul.

"Christie and I are doing everything in our power to make this wedding a memorable event for her and Jake." I frowned. "The only thing is the flowers and vines will cover most of the details during the wedding. It's such a shame to hide your work."

Henri grinned. "I knew that when I designed it. During the wedding, it will serve as a wedding arch, but afterward you can string it with lights or a vine can climb over it. Whatever suits you. I'm sure Elsi will have some good ideas. She's got a magical touch. Like a fairy godmother, that one, but for gardens. She'll be at the wedding, won't she?"

I couldn't help but notice the twinkle in Henri's eyes when he mentioned my mother, but was that just because Sofia had teased her earlier? They were old friends, after all. When my father and Henri's wife, Gladys, were still alive, they used to get together to play bridge or go bowling. After their respective spouses had died, Mom and Henri spent less time together. "Yes, of course. She wouldn't miss it. And you're attending?"

Henri nodded. "Annabelle's altered a suit for me, and James took me shopping for a fresh shirt and tie. I'm ready for the big day. Save a dance for me?"

"With pleasure." I smiled at his enthusiasm. I took a moment to study the wedding arch. Henri knew the assignment, and he had nailed it. Literally. "Do you think James can bring the arch over to Hygge House for me?" I asked, glancing to where he was still chatting with Sally. There was no way I was going to get that thing home with Tuuli in my little trailer, even if Hugo jogged beside me.

"Of course. Now that Tyler's here, James is free to go." Henri pointed to two pots with hostas. "Elsi mentioned she wanted something for the side of the house. Bring those to her, too."

"How much do I owe you?" I asked, pulling out my phone case with my debit card. I'd paid for the arch in advance, but it occurred to me it was worth much more than Henri had charged me. Plus, we owed him for the hostas.

Henri waved his hand. "Put your money away. They're a gift for Elsi."

I thanked him again and followed James to his truck as he carried the wooden structure and placed it gently in his cab. He nestled the hostas between the arch and the side of the cab, careful that they wouldn't jostle too much as he drove.

"Do you think Elsi has any leftover pancakes?" James asked, closing the cab door with a thud. "Or some coffee?"

"I can arrange that for you, especially since you're delivering this precious cargo. Meet you there?"

"You don't want a ride? I could get Tuuli in the back with the trailer if I cover the arch with a blanket." James surveyed the back of his truck.

"No need. I'll feel better if we don't risk it. This arch is too important. If we damage it, we'll break Henri's heart and devastate Grace. And imagine Christie's reaction! You don't need her wrath." We both laughed.

"You're right. Christie would have my head if anything happened to the arch, and I don't know how I'd explain it to Dad."

"And Grace certainly doesn't need more stress right now."

James frowned and crossed his arms over his plaid shirt. "Is everything okay with the bride?" he asked, genuine concern in his voice. "She's not having second thoughts, is she?"

I looked behind me, conscious that everyone in the garden centre was aware of Grace's upcoming nuptials and might even be guests. "I'm not sure. She was upset at her dress fitting. I mean, she loved the dress, but she was overly emotional, I guess."

"Does it have to do with her brother, do you think?" James asked. "I mean, it hasn't been that long since he ... died."

"That was my first thought, but even Christie's having difficulty getting her to decide on anything. Like she's stalling or something. Or having second thoughts about the wedding." If Grace didn't want to get married, we'd all have to support her decision, but I didn't want another big event getting cancelled at Hygge House.

"Give her time." James opened the door to his truck. "Let's focus on getting the place ready. Grace will come around. Pre-wedding jitters are normal."

"I hope you're right." James's calm tone was reassuring, and I felt better about the whole thing. Besides, there wasn't anything I could do. If Grace cancelled the wedding, we'd just have to deal with her decision.

"Did you have cold feet before your wedding?" James asked, a curious expression on his face.

"No. I was absolutely certain that I wanted to get married. Peter did, too. We were both so young and sure of ourselves. It would have been better if we'd slowed down. Of course, then I wouldn't have Sofia." I contemplated the decisions I'd made in my life. Peter wasn't the man for me in the end, but that didn't mean we didn't have some good years. "What about you?"

"Nope. I proposed to someone once, and we were engaged for a few months, but in the end, we agreed to part ways. Probably for the best, I reckon." He flashed his charming smile at me.

With Hugo in the trailer, I pedalled Tuuli away from the hardware store, giving a quick wave to Henri before turning onto the street, aware that James was following behind.

By the time I reached Hygge House, I was hot and sweaty, and this time it wasn't just because of hot flashes. Summer was really upon us. I parked Tuuli in her usual spot beside the garden shed, and Hugo jumped out and bounded toward James, who was already discussing the positioning of the wedding arch with my mother.

"Why, it's just perfect, Minna. Look at all those lovely details. Your father has really outdone himself, James."

"Dad thought you'd appreciate all the garden and fairy-tale references." James pointed out different varieties of flowers and leaves carved into the wood, along with fairies and garden sprites. "And he sent you the hostas for the side of the house."

"Good man," Mom said. "I'll get those planted this afternoon."

"I'll carry them out to the garden for you, Elsi," James said.

"Do you need help here, Mom?" I asked. I sneezed and searched my pockets for a tissue.

"No, darling. Are you alright? You're not getting sick, are you? Summer colds are the absolute worst." Mom tilted her head and gave me that motherly look of concern. She reached for my forehead with the back of her hand. She remembered I was in my fifties, didn't she? "Your forehead is hot."

"My whole body is always hot, Mom. Menopause, remember?"

Mom waved scoffed. "I don't know what you're talking about. I didn't have any symptoms at all."

"Okay, Mom." I was sure Mom either didn't remember or was in denial.

When James returned, I invited him in for coffee and pancake leftovers. And I could cool down before we got back to preparing the rooms for the upcoming guests. This wedding was a great excuse to get Hygge House into shape.

Now that the wedding arch was in place, I could see it all coming together. A garden in full bloom, wedding chairs ordered and to be delivered the day before the ceremony. The deck near the lake would provide a suitable surface for dancing, and a place for the band to set up. This wedding would surely be one to remember, and maybe even fulfil Grace's idea of a midsummer fairy tale.

Chapter 3

On Monday, James arrived early to work on the upstairs rooms, focussing on repairs to the floorboards, trim, and window sills while I made my way through the guest rooms that had already been painted. I'd chosen light and neutral tones inspired by nature, and each room had its own ambience. I'd had the foresight to order new beds when we first moved into Hygge House, and purchased bedspreads and cushions, as well as new rugs.

As I put the finishing touches on the room that once—and still—belonged to our resident ghost, Fanny, I caught a slight chill. The drapes moved slightly at the window overlooking the circular driveway at the front of the house.

Our real estate agent, Derek, had told us Fanny was friendly, and so far I believed him, but according to my mother, she was very active. I moved toward the window. It was slightly ajar, so a breeze from outside was surely responsible. I didn't believe in ghosts, but every now and again a cold spot in the house, or movement at the corner of my eye, made me rethink my position.

"Everything okay up here?" Mom asked, pausing at the bedroom door. She wore a light summer dress with a smock, and her signature wide-brimmed hat on her silver bob. I glanced down at my paint-splattered shorts and t-shirt. Mom's attire was straight out of a garden magazine. I sighed.

"Making progress. But I'm not feeling great. Didn't have a good sleep. Too much tossing and turning."

"It's that summer cold I warned you about. Take some echinacea and get some rest."

"No, I don't think I'm sick. Just worried about the wedding. We still have a lot to do, and it's so soon."

"It's all coming along, Minna. No need to worry." Mom took a few steps into Fanny's room and scanned the space, her hands on her hips. "My word. You've done a beautiful job. I think I might want to move into this space after the wedding."

"Thanks, Mom." I plumped the last pillow and placed it on a vintage chair in the corner. "I'm happy with how it turned out. But what would Fanny say about you taking over her room?" I smiled to think a ghost would have an opinion.

"Oh, no worries. She'd love it." Mom moved towards the curtains. "Perhaps not the curtains so much, but she can live with them."

I laughed out loud. "Really? Fanny's giving you messages about decor from the great beyond?"

Mom shrugged. "Just conveying the message." She sauntered out of the room and paused in the hallway before heading to talk to Astrid—who sat a safe distance from Fanny's room, but looked decidedly uncomfortable—before going down the grand staircase to the first floor and then, I presumed, out to the garden.

Could my mother really communicate with the ghost of the former resident? I shivered and closed the door quietly behind me so as not to disturb anything or anyone inside the room. "Don't look at me like that, Astrid. You're going to have to make friends with whoever stays here, whether it's Fanny or someone else." In fact, Lillian Alcott, Jack's mother, would be the first guest to stay in the room. I hoped Fanny wouldn't mind having a roommate.

James popped his head out from the next room before stepping into the hallway. "I thought I heard your voice. This room is ready for painting. If you're up to it."

"Yeah, I don't really have a choice. There are only ten days before the guests arrive, and these rooms need to be ready." I wiped my brow and sighed, feeling a chill pass through me.

"Are you feeling okay? You look a little pale." James leaned against the doorframe, concern flitting across his face. Did I look so terrible that even James would comment on it?

I didn't want to trouble him with all of our Hygge House problems. He already had to troubleshoot issues with the renovation; he shouldn't have to worry about our events. But James was so understanding, it was easy to confide in him.

"I'm fine. Tired, mostly. And I guess I'm a little stressed out. These rooms need to be done, and the garden isn't quite ready, and Christie doesn't have a confirmed guest list, so Michael is having a fit because he doesn't know how much food he needs, and well, the ripple effect continues." I sat on the top stair and put my head in my hands, restraining my welling tears. It wasn't like me to cry, but menopause had brought with it many unexpected emotions, and they came at the least convenient times.

James strode over and sat beside me on the top step, his knee touching mine, and swung an arm around my shoulder. He said nothing, and that was just perfect. Just let me sit and breathe and lean against him. He didn't offer to solve my problems, but I appreciated his listening to them.

After a few moments, I sat straighter and smiled. "Right. On with it." I'd need to muster every bit of energy I had to push through to the end, but as I stood up, my head swam, and I grabbed the bannister for balance.

"Hey, Minna. I have an idea. Why don't I take you for a ride on the boat this evening? Take your mind off things for a few hours."

"Love to," I said, and meant it. The thought of an evening cruising with James sounded divine. It had been ages since I'd been out on the lake. We'd been too busy this spring, and our brief visits to Lakewood over the years rarely gave us a chance to get out there. Besides, my ex-husband Peter didn't care for boating, so there was that.

I needed a break from the work, and being near the water always calmed my nerves. With that, we parted ways. I went to the storage room for the next room's can of paint and clean brushes, and James headed down the hall to work on the third room. Knowing James, he'd make sure the rooms were in perfect condition for the wedding guests. I just needed to keep up the pace.

That evening, James swung by the dock at Hygge House in his Stanley—a workhorse of a boat he used for hauling materials to lakefront cottages he worked on and, more often than not, fishing. It was still light out, but I carried a sweater in case it cooled off. The lake was calm, and I watched the ripples move toward the shore as we pulled away. Within minutes, Hygge House was in the distance, and my worries had melted away.

"You mentioned Grace might have cold feet about the wedding." James navigated along the shore at a pace that was perfect for watching waterfowl and sneaking peeks at the camps and cottages along the shore. Many of the older camps had been there since before I was born, but others had been torn down in favour of all-year round cottages, sometimes bought up by wealthy southerners.

"It's not cold feet exactly, but she's definitely worried about something, and neither Christie nor I have figured it out. I suspect it has something to do with Jack." I shrugged and sat back in my seat, admiring the view. Despite their compatibility, Christie and Jack sometimes argued, but that seemed normal enough.

James nodded. "Jack mentioned his friends were having a stag party on Friday night for him. I was a bit surprised, but he invited me. I guess he figures one more old guy won't make a difference." He laughed.

"You're not that old." I nudged him on the shoulder.

"Not that young, either." He smiled. "Jack wants to introduce me to his Uncle Rick, but he wasn't sure if Rick would come to the stag or not. He looked disappointed about it. I was hoping to meet him. Pretty sure I saw him play in their band when I was a kid."

"Hmm. That's part of the problem. Christie can't get the final numbers, and if some of Jack's relatives are holding out on the RSVP, I can see why Grace would be upset." I crossed my arms and leaned back in my chair, staring out at the water. "To be honest, I'll be relieved when the wedding is over. It's been a tough one, what with not having the house completely ready and the short timelines."

"Having regrets?" James asked, navigating along the shoreline.

"No, it's just been a lot. I guess I'm a little tired and haven't quite recovered from all the events of the past few months." A chill passed over me and I grabbed my sweater, but I wasn't sure if it was the thought of Owen Bradshaw's dead body on the breakfast nook floor, or the cooling evening air. No one talks about the effects on a person after a mystery gets solved. Did Jessica Fletcher ever get run-down or have bad dreams? I doubted it.

James grabbed a blanket and handed it to me. "Don't get a chill. The last thing you need is to get sick before the wedding."

"You sound like my mother." I pulled the blanket around my shoulders.

"Elsi is a wise woman. You should listen to her." James grinned.

We sat in silence while the boat carved its way toward the channel. As it narrowed and then widened again, James swung us around an island with a cottage I'd always admired. Last I heard, a family of Americans shared it.

We headed back along the opposite shore as daylight faded. The cottages and camps along the shoreline started glowing. Everything looked serene and safe. In the distance, the lights from Driftwood Cottages glimmered, and I remembered the beach where Christie and I had swum as kids.

"Ever spend time at Driftwood Beach?" I asked, leaning to get a closer view. It had changed little in all the years I'd been away.

"All the time when I was a kid," James said, slowing down and drifting past. "Did you hear about the teen who disappeared from that beach maybe thirty or forty years ago? Locals recovered her body farther down the lake. Current probably took her. I think she was a tourist."

I shivered again, imagining her fright, and the terror of her family. A parent's worst nightmare. "Mom always warned us to be careful and not go out too far, especially after that incident."

As we neared Hygge House, I caught my breath. The warm lights from the house glowed, the string lights around the garden twinkled, and orbs along the footpath sparkled. "It's so beautiful. The last time I felt this way about the house was the first day we toured it. Remember?"

"I remember you weren't so sure about buying it." He turned off the engine, and we sat in silence, the boat gently rocking as we admired the property from the lake. It was the first time I'd seen it from this vantage point, and it really was stunning.

I laughed. "That's true. Christie kept it a secret right until the end. But she was right, of course. There's something magical about this place. Sometimes I feel like a princess living in a castle. Other days, I feel more like Cinderella—mopping floors, paintings rooms, doing laundry."

"People don't realize what goes into making a castle a home—and a business. But it is the perfect location for a garden wedding." James turned the engine back on and manoeuvred the boat to the dock. As I stepped out, Hugo bounded towards me from the house, more excited to see me than any person ever could be.

"I needed that little getaway. Thanks, James." I handed him the blanket he kept in the boat. It had helped, but hadn't prevented the chill from settling deep into my body.

"Anytime. And Minna? Don't worry so much about this wedding. The house is in great shape, and Elsi's garden looks amazing. You've got this, okay?"

I nodded. "Yeah, we've got this." I said goodnight and watched him pull away from the dock, headed towards his small lakeshore cottage to the east of Hygge House, before plodding along the lit footpath toward the kitchen nook—the very one where I'd found the body—taking a deep breath before opening the door. Despite the warmth of the house, I still felt cold, so I made some tea and brought it up to my room.

An hour later, wrapped in heavy blankets, my head bursting with a headache, I ached with chills. The timing couldn't be worse. I drifted off, hoping I would wake up feeling better in the morning. There was too much to be done to get sick, and I couldn't rely on James and Christie to do everything for me.

Chapter 4

To my chagrin, I didn't feel better the next morning. In fact, I woke with an intense pain in my body and a temperature that swung from too hot to too cold. My blankets were a puddle at the end of the bed, twisted from my constant movement.

A light knock on the door could only be my daughter. Sofia opened the door and cocked her head slightly, her eyebrows knitted together. "You look terrible, Mom."

"Thanks a lot." I stifled a cough. I tried to smile, but even my facial muscles hurt.

"I'm going to work at Nordic Cozy. Do you need anything before I leave?" Sofia looked concerned, but I didn't want to trouble her. Or get her sick.

"I'll be okay. Have a good day at work. What about your mummu? What's she doing today?"

"She's already in the garden. She'll have everything potted and pruned before that wedding if she has to work day and night." Sofia smiled fondly. "She's complaining that there must be a fox lurking around the place, but I haven't seen one. Have you?" Since moving to Lakewood, my mother and daughter had really bonded. It made our decision to move into Hygge House together that much sweeter.

"Not near the house, but I saw one cross Mosquito Trail the other day when I was walking Hugo. Beautiful thing, but it wouldn't do to have him close to the house or digging in Mummu's garden."

Sofia nodded. "I'll pick up some cold meds on my way home. Text me if you need anything."

"Thanks, kulta," I said, closing my eyes to the light of the morning, too bright for my eyes and head. I felt Hugo's warm body curled up at my feet. Freya was sleeping on my sweater in the chair by my bed. Astrid, as usual, was nowhere to be seen. I kind of admired her. She didn't need anyone or anything, and if she did, it was always on her terms.

Sofia left me to my misery, and I drifted in and out of sleep until my phone buzzed and woke me again some time later.

"Christie?" I asked. She normally texted, so a phone call surprised me. "Everything okay?"

"Okay? No, it's not okay. I'm furious." Christie was usually calm under pressure. Nothing fazed that woman. "You sound terrible, by the way. Are you still sleeping? I know you're not a morning person, but this is even late for you. What's going on?"

"I was going to ask the same of you." I propped myself up on my pillows. When was the last time Christie was upset about anything? Okay, besides the murder in the kitchen nook three months ago. That was not a highlight of our decades-long friendship.

"Right. I'll start. I've been having difficulty getting Grace to commit to decisions and texting Jack for his input hasn't led me anywhere. He just says, 'ask Grace.' So, this morning, Grace texted to tell me Jack's uncle, Richard, is back on the guest list and he now needs a room. But we're all full at Hygge House, right?"

"Yeah, Jack's mom and his siblings are staying here with their kids, and Grace's maid of honour is coming from out of town, too." I coughed. "We gave Richard Alcott's room to the best man, Harry. You'll have to find him a room at Driftwood Cottages or else disappoint Harry." Grace had already agreed that any out-of-town guests could stay there, while immediate family or folks standing in the wedding party should be at Hygge House. Thank goodness it was a smallish event.

"Yeah, okay. I'm on it. No point in moving Harry. Besides, Richard's not standing in the wedding, even though he is family. Who knows if he'll even turn up," Christie said, taking a deep breath. "Apparently, the man just can't decide what he wants to do."

"Still furious?" I asked, reaching for my nearly empty tissue box.

"No," she conceded. "I wasn't actually angry, but it's our first wedding at Hygge House, and I just want it to be perfect, you know? Sorry to lay this all on you. You're probably feeling as stressed as I am. But forget about me. How are *you*?" Christie's voice was more relaxed now. She just needed to let off some steam.

"Not to worry. I have a bit of a cold or something, but I'm sure it's nothing. I'll be back on my feet in no time. The only problem is that I can't paint today, and that puts me behind schedule. But don't worry. It's going to be fine," I added, not wanting to give her another problem to deal with.

I could almost hear Christie running ideas through her head and see her clipboard in her hand. "Okay, I got it. You hold tight and get some rest. I'll take care of everything. See you soon."

Before I could say anything, she had hung up. I turned off my ringer, grabbed my covers and pulled them up before slumping back down. The chill had returned. Hugo sighed and shifted, snuggling into the crook of my knees. Before I knew it, I was out.

A few hours later, a woman's hushed tones in the hallway startled me awake. Even Hugo's ears perked up, and he stared at the door, emitting a low growl. It was unlike Hugo to vocalize. It could only mean one thing. Someone or something was out there.

Making as little sound as possible, I sat up in bed and strained to hear the voice. Was I dreaming? Perhaps it was Fanny, believing no one could hear her. I pulled my covers off and slipped my feet into my red felt slippers, inching toward my door. I hadn't bothered to lock it. That was clearly a mistake.

I opened the door a crack but could see no one in the long hallway, but the voice was louder. The door to Fanny's room—we all called it that now—was ajar, but I distinctly remembered closing it. Was this some kind of fever dream? Hugo jumped off the bed and followed at my heels as I tiptoed towards the space, barely able to breathe. It wasn't Mom's voice, and it definitely wasn't Christie's. Sofia was at work, so it was just me left on my own with Hugo, and he sensed something was wrong, too.

With my fingertips, I gently nudged the door. The opening widened. I caught my breath and stepped back, letting out a surprised squeal.

"Oh! It's you," I said, finally able to get words out. My shoulders dropped, and my heart rate slowed.

Sarah Bean stood near Fanny's window, holding a brown paper bag in one hand and a coffee cup in the other. Across from her, James eyed me with a questioning look, probably suppressing his laughter, or perhaps critiquing my choice of bedclothes. Mom had given me a long white nightgown that looked straight out of the Victorian era, and I'd taken to wearing it instead of my beat-up old pajama bottoms and t-shirt.

Sarah's eyes widened. "I'm sorry, Minna. Did we wake you up? We came in here so we wouldn't disturb you." She frowned. "I guess that didn't really work."

"I've been in and out all day. Weird dreams, so when I heard a voice, I thought ..." I hesitated to tell Sarah about Fanny. I didn't really believe in spirits, but judging by my behaviour, maybe Fanny was changing my mind.

"You thought what?" James prompted, his smile widening.

"Nothing ... I just had to investigate. I thought I was alone in the house." I shot him a look, as if to tell him to keep it quiet, but truthfully, it didn't matter. Besides Fanny, my mother swore Owen

Bradshaw haunted the grounds now, though we had no evidence of that whatsoever. She was probably just pulling my leg. Even as a kid, I could never tell if she was making up stories about garden fairies and sauna elves, or if she really believed what she was saying.

"Well, I brought you some of Brian's chicken noodle soup and fresh bread, and—"

"Coffee! You're a saint." I reached out for the cup. "I must be feeling better because this smells divine. And so does the soup." I thanked her profusely. We hadn't been friends for long, but Sarah and Brian Bean were the kinds of folks you could rely on, and a genuinely nice young couple. Boreal Beanery was easily my favourite place for great coffee, and they were quickly becoming some of my favourite people.

"I hope you feel better soon." Sarah touched my arm briefly. She handed me the bag with the soup and bread, and my appetite returned. "Brian should be here soon," she added.

"Brian?" I asked, glancing from Sarah to James.

"Yeah, he offered to come and paint. James told us you have a pretty tight deadline for your rooms up here. This one looks amazing, by the way. Besides, Christie's enlisting the troops, and when she calls, we answer."

"I appreciate that. And thank you so much for the food."

"Anytime." Sarah headed towards the staircase. "I have to get back to the shop. Just text if you need anything else. "

"Will do." As the front door opened and closed, I turned to James. "Did you know anything about this?" I held up the coffee and the bag. "And what about Brian? Did you enlist him too?"

James shrugged, a sheepish grin on his face. "People around here help one another. You were in the bit city for too long and forgot what being a good neighbour means."

He was right. I'd been so focussed on getting Hygge House renovated and decorated for our events—not to mention solving a crime—that I'd forgotten how the town had pulled together for us. And here they were, doing it again.

"Listen, I have work to do, and you need to rest. Go have your soup before it cools off, but save me one of those salty caramel chocolate chip cookies, would you?"

I glanced into the bag, my mouth watering at the thought of them. "I'm making no promises, but come down for coffee when you're ready."

Whatever had made me feel so unwell was still making me drag my feet, but I made it to the main floor just in time to meet Tyler, Henri, and Brian, paintbrushes in hand, and smiles on their faces. Lakewood folks would always save the day.

Chapter 5

By Saturday, I had no trace of the bug I'd contracted and my energy was nearly back, but it was going to be a big day with Grace's bridal shower on the agenda for the afternoon. I poured myself a second cup of coffee and checked the time on the clock in the kitchen, conscious that we only had another hour before guests would arrive.

The front door chimed, and I padded down the hall, passing by Stuga, where Sofia and my mother were arranging flowers. Because Grace's bridal shower was going to be so small, we wanted to host it in our more intimate space, which doubled as our family living room. The comfortable furniture, feature fireplace, and large windows made it both relaxing and inviting. Perfect for this gathering.

"Are you getting the door, Minna?" Mom asked, holding a bouquet from the garden in one hand and secateurs in her other hand. "I hope that's the cake delivery. They're late today."

"On my way," I said, taking a sip of coffee. Amanda had promised to deliver the cake from Fika and Frosting earlier that morning. What was holding her up? I hoped they weren't having a problem with it. The cake was the centrepiece of the entire event, and we wanted to wow Grace with it.

I pulled open the door to find Christie struggling under the weight of a large box, and Amanda behind her with another one that must contain the cake.

"Took you long enough." Christie jostled her way into the entrance. She didn't sound upset, and she followed it with an apology. "Sorry I'm late. I slept in."

"That will teach you to work too hard and try to save the day. You really didn't need to take on everything. I wasn't sick for *that* long."

I ushered them both towards Stuga.

"You're not getting the bug, are you?" I asked, taking the box out of Christie's arms. It wasn't like her to sleep in. If anyone, that would be me. I was definitely not a morning person, but Christie was like the Energizer Bunny.

"No, I'm fine. I just stayed up late trying to sort out the details for next weekend." She suppressed a yawn. "I think it's all settled now. My charts are flowing and my spreadsheets are adding up."

Mom looked up when we came in and spied Amanda. "Oh good! The cake is here. I was worried you'd forgotten all about it."

"I would never forget something as important as this, Elsi," Amanda said, taking no offense at my mother's remarks. These days, Mom said what she thought more often, and it sometimes appeared rude, but not to the people who knew and loved her. It could be charming or offensive, depending on one's mood.

"We created a spot here for it." Sofia had already laid out our white dessert plates and silverware, plus coffee and teacups on a table I'd found at Vintage Pier.

Amanda put the box down on the coffee table and gently lifted the cake out. A round of oohs and aahs followed.

It was a three-tiered round cake with white icing and decorated with tiny handmade flowers and little circles of silver balls in the shape of wreaths. It was both elegant and whimsical. Amanda placed it down on the table and stepped back, crossing her arms, tilting her head as she examined it, and then adjusted it slightly.

"Terri really outdid herself this time." Amanda clearly admired her partner's work. So did I.

"Amanda, you must tell Terri that her work is simply stunning." Mom leaned in to get a closer look at the design. "The flowers are so delicate."

Amanda beamed. "Well, Elsi. You can tell her yourself, because she'll be here in an hour. She had to change after spending the morning on the cake." Amanda's tone was pleasant, but she'd clearly got Mom's message about being late and was reminding her of the work that had gone into making it.

The door chimed again, and I glanced at the clock. Too early for guests to arrive. I still needed to change out of my joggers and t-shirt. "Christie, could you get it?" I asked. "I really need to get dressed."

Christie's hair and makeup were perfect as always, and she had donned a lovely pale green wrap dress. She made dressing look stylish and effortless. I followed her toward the front door, but made a beeline up the stairs to change.

I heard two voices on the porch when Christie opened the door, and I paused on the staircase. One was male and the other female, and it sounded like they were deep into an argument.

"Sorry, Christie." Grace sounded flustered. "Jack was just dropping me off. He has plans to go fishing for the afternoon with some of his friends, so I'm a little early. I hope that's okay."

"Of course, it is. You're the guest of honour, and today is all about you. You can do whatever pleases you," Christie said. I smiled to myself at her generous tone. The bride's early arrival was not part of her detailed checklist. "Is everything okay?"

I couldn't see them from my spot on the stairs, but Grace's hesitation spoke volumes. I made my way back down the stairs and greeted them both. Christie glanced at me. If there were a problem, we needed to deal with it now.

I glanced down the hall behind me. "Why don't we sit for a minute?" I suggested. I stepped outside and led them to the covered verandah. Grace and Jack sat beside each other on the rattan couch, and Christie and I took chairs across from them.

I leaned in with my hands clasped on my knees. "I couldn't help but overhear you arguing. Is there anything we can do?"

Grace breathed deeply, and her eyes welled with tears. "I'm not sure. It's just been so stressful."

Jack reached for her hand, shifting uncomfortably beside her.

"The wedding preparations?" Christie asked. "It's always stressful, especially for the bride. And I'm sorry if I've contributed to that with all my texts and phone calls."

"No, it's not that," Grace took a tissue out of her purse and wiped her nose, glancing at Jack.

Jack cleared his throat and hung his head. "I'm afraid it's my family. We're having some ... difficulties in communication, you could say."

I nodded, waiting for him to tell us more.

"The plan was for my mother to stay at Hygge House, along with my brother Ian, his wife, and their daughter." Jack directed his attention to Christie.

She nodded. "Yes, I have Lillian in one room, Ian, Kate and Rosie in another. Plus, I have the maid of honour—" Christie glanced at her clipboard, "Eloise—in the third room, and your best man, Harry, in the fourth. That leaves the bridal suite for you and Grace."

"That's right. Harry's room was originally for my Uncle Rick." Jack shook his head.

Grace squeezed Jack's hand. "Richard Alcott was like a father to Jack growing up. When his father died, Jack was only eleven. Uncle Rick was everything to him." Grace shook her head. "He said he was coming, and then said he wasn't sure. And now this."

Christie and I exchanged glances. "It's not a problem. I booked him a place at Driftwood Cottages. It's not in the house with the rest of you, but it's not too far away, and the cottages are really lovely."

Jack shook his head. "Driftwood is fine. It's not about the room."

"What do you mean?" I asked. "What's the problem?"

Jack pulled out his cellphone and scrolled, pausing on a text message. He held out his phone, and I took it, while Christie leaned toward me to read the message.

**Jack, I'm sorry I can't be there for your big day.
Better for me not to disturb the past.**

Christie frowned. "What does he mean?"

"That's the problem. We're not sure." Grace crossed and uncrossed her legs. "And now he's not answering Jack's texts."

Jack reached across the table for his cellphone. What could Richard Alcott be worried about? What happened in the past?

"And your family members have mentioned nothing that Richard might be concerned about?" I asked.

Jack shook his head. "I've always had a great relationship with Uncle Rick, and he's met Grace a few times. They hit it off right away. Honestly, I haven't asked Ian or my mom yet, but I probably should."

"That's a good idea," I said. "In the meantime, let's keep Rick's cottage in case he changes his mind. He seems conflicted. You never know, he might come despite that text." I glanced at my watch. "I hate to do this, but our guests are coming soon."

Jack smiled. "I get it. The groom is unwanted. I'll be back to pick you up. I'll reach out to Ian and see if he's heard anything, but Grace, don't mention it to my mom, okay? Not yet."

Grace agreed and gave him a quick kiss. There was no opportunity to ask him why he didn't want his mom to know. I put that in my back pocket, curious about what was going on with this family. While Christie ushered Grace into the house, I ran upstairs to change, pulling out a pale blue skirt and top for the occasion.

By the time I returned to Stuga, Sofia was pouring coffee for Grace. Mom was reorganizing the couch cushions, and Christie was checking the checklist on her clipboard one more time. It was the top of the hour, and everything was ready for Grace's bridal shower.

As the guests trickled in bearing gifts and good cheer, I relaxed for the first time in weeks. Everything was just as it should be: Grace was all smiles, Christie was directing without being bossy, Sofia was taking pictures and videos, and Elsi was in fine form chatting up guests. And on the table, Terri's specialty cake drew admiration and was the focus of many photographs.

I moved to the table and poured coffee and tea, thankful the bride was happy and her future mother-in-law, Lillian, appeared to be having a good time.

After opening the gifts—many purchased from Grace's registry at Nordic Cozy—Mom and Sophia served cake and the ladies chatted among themselves. I sat next to Kate, Jack's sister-in-law, eager to get to know her a little.

"Your first time in Lakewood?" I asked.

Kate nodded. "Rick told us about growing up here with Ian's dad, Patrick, and Ian always wanted to visit, but we never got around to it. I don't know; maybe memories of his father made it difficult. It's not like Kingston is that far away, but still ..."

"I understand. I lost my father when I was young, too. He's everywhere in this town. How's Ian holding up?"

"Really well, actually. He's enjoyed seeing the sights with Rosie, and telling us stories about his dad." Kate beamed. "I'm happy that Ian is part of the wedding party. He's older than Jack, you see, so he moved out for school when Jack was still pretty young, and then we got married. Lillian raised Jack on her own."

I nodded and took a sip of coffee. "And Uncle Rick? Was he part of the family, too?"

"Yes, of course. He moved to Kingston from Toronto when Patrick died to be closer to them. He was always around for Ian and Jack, but Jack really took a shine to him. I guess he needed a dad, and Richard was there for him."

"That's so lovely. Do you expect him to appear this weekend?" I asked gently, not knowing how much Kate knew about the situation.

She frowned and leaned toward me. "I don't know what's going on. He can't seem to decide, and we don't know why. I suspect he didn't want to come back to Lakewood. Maybe memories of his brother Patrick—their father—are too painful for him."

I smiled and offered her more coffee. Kate shook her head and turned her attention to Rosie, who was playing with Hugo nearby. Kate could be right, and Richard didn't want to return to the place of his youth. They say you can never go home again. In his case, it might be true.

Chapter 6

A few hours later, the last of the guests had hugged Grace and congratulated her again before heading out, leaving Grace and Jack's family with us. Rosie was trying to entice Astrid to play with some ribbon, but she remained unmoved, while Freya frolicked on the floor beside her.

I surveyed the room. Brightly coloured wrapping paper and enormous bows strewn on the floor, plates with crumbs of cake, and cups with half-finished cups of coffee and tea scattered around the space. Christie sank into an armchair across from Grace.

I puttered around, gathering the wrapping debris while Sofia and Kate collected the dishes. Elsi sat beside Lillian on the couch, deep in conversation about who knows what. It was nice to see my mother connect with Lillian. She had a lot of friends in town, but a new acquaintance was always welcome and had fresh stories to share.

"How are you feeling, Grace?" Christie asked.

Grace smiled. "Everything was perfect, thanks to all of you." She seemed genuinely pleased, and I was relieved. Grace's phone pinged, and she glanced at her screen. "Jack's here. He wants to take us out to dinner," she said, turning to Lillian.

"Lovely, dear," Lillian said, standing up. "It was wonderful to meet you, and I'm looking forward to the big day. Better not keep Jack waiting too long, Grace."

Grace agreed and started gathering her belongings. "Oh, there are so many gifts. I can't believe it." She appeared a little flustered at the thought of organizing it all.

"You go on ahead. We'll gather up the gifts and deliver them to Jack's car," I suggested. "I'll get Sofia to box up the rest of the cake."

Grace agreed. "That would be perfect, Minna," she said, relief flooding her features. She followed Lillian out, with Kate and Rosie following behind, thanking us again for the event.

"I think that's everything," I placed the last gift in a box. Sofia, Christie and I filled our arms and headed outside, a bit like Santa's helpers but on a beautiful warm day. Lillian waved as she entered Kate's car, and Rosie jumped into the back seat. They headed down the lane, and I felt suddenly relieved. They were lovely people, but we were definitely on show today. I hoped we'd passed their test.

Jack and Grace were in the car, but the doors were still open. We heard their raised voices.

"Do you think we should turn around?" Sofia asked. She adjusted the cake box in her arms. It would be a disaster for the rest of the cake to land on the driveway.

Christie shook her head. "Nope. Let's just get these in the car, and they can go on with their ... discussion."

I agreed and followed Christie towards the couple. Their voices were getting louder.

"Jack, you need to let it go. If he doesn't want to come, that's up to him."

"Why wouldn't he come? He won't answer my texts or calls, and Ian said he doesn't get what's going on either." Jack slammed a fist into the roof of his car. Grace flinched.

"Can we just let it go? The wedding's in a week." Grace's voice pleaded.

I cleared my throat, hoping they'd notice us standing with arms laden. Already, my muscles ached. I hadn't quite gotten my energy back after being sick all week.

"Oh, sorry." Jack rushed to take the box out of my hands. Grace opened the trunk and pushed the seats down. Sofia and Christie handed Jack the other boxes to arrange, and he slammed the trunk door down.

"I guess you heard all that?" Grace asked. "We didn't mean to get into it again." Not for the first time, Grace's faced look flushed.

"No worries," Christie said. "Listen, I've run a lot of events over the years, and weddings can be the most stressful. Family members don't always do what's expected or what's needed. My suggestion? Forget him and enjoy this special time together. If he changes his mind, your Uncle Rick will have the best time. If he doesn't, he'll be missing out on your wedding, but that doesn't mean he's less important to you."

I nodded along with Christie's speech, admiring her ability to impart perspective. Whether Jack and Grace would listen was an entirely separate thing.

Jack crossed his arms and nodded solemnly. He paused, and I held my breath. "You know what? I agree. Uncle Rick has never let me down before. If he's not coming, he must have his reasons. I just have to make peace with that."

Grace was visibly relieved. Jack thanked us and sat in the driver's seat. Grace gave Christie a quick hug and thanked us all again for the shower. "I love what you said, Christie. I hope Jack takes it on board. He can get very passionate about things. I guess that's why I love him."

"Everything will be fine." I squeezed her hand. Grace nodded and sat in the car, waving her hand out the window as they pulled away.

Sofia shook her head. "Is that relationship going to work out? Those two argue all the time. And his uncle isn't making it any easier on them." I wondered if Sofia was remembering Peter and me fighting in the years before our divorce. How had that affected her relationships? So far, everything was going well with Tyler, but disagreements were part of being a couple. At least sometimes.

"Who knows? Relationships are hard, but lots of people make it for decades and decades. Just look at Sally and Sean Murphy. Sixty years together and still going strong," I said.

"You might be right, Sofia," Christie said. "All we can do is hope for the best and plan for the worst."

Ugh. How could we plan when we knew the worst was something no one should have to experience? Hoping for the best was more my speed.

Chapter 7

We spent Sunday tidying up after the bridal shower and finishing the last-minute details for the upcoming wedding. Christie had booked a meeting with Floyd Beck, Northern Spirit's leader and bass player, for first thing Monday morning. The day came too soon, but by the time he arrived, Hugo and I had already had our morning walk on the trails, and I was on my second cup of joe.

"Nice to meet you in person," Floyd said, holding out a long-fingered hand to shake Christie's.

Christie took his hand, and he squeezed it, holding it longer than one might expect. I tried to hide my smirk.

"Why don't we go into the Aurora Room?" Christie suggested. She led Floyd, and I followed behind with Hugo Dogberg at my heels. Floyd's long, dark hair, streaked with strands of grey, was remarkably shiny. I examined the tattoos on his long arms and the way he ambled, wondering how he kept his body from toppling over with the long curve in his back. He probably wasn't much older than I was, but it was hard to tell with these rock and roll types.

We sat at the table Christie had set up for the purpose, her clipboard and erasable pen ready in front of her. Hugo jumped onto my lap and licked my chin.

"Sorry it's taken so long to stop by. The band has been on a northern tour and just got back."

"That's impressive," I said. "Do you tour a lot these days?"

Floyd shook his head. "Jed, our guitarist, has a load of kids, and his wife doesn't like him being away. I don't blame her. Our drummer, Zander, is working all the time, and Norah—she's our vocalist—doesn't want to travel much anymore. But we still try to tour once a year, at least."

"We don't want to take too much of your time," Christie said, meaning she was conscious of *our* time. She glanced at her checklist. "So, you're okay for the rehearsal dinner to play a few songs and then, for the wedding, to set up near the lake for dancing? James built the dance floor, and there's a platform for the band."

"You got it, honey. Whatever you need," Floyd said, winking at her. I could see Christie shift uncomfortably, but she smiled.

"And do you have the list of songs that the bride and groom requested?" Christie asked, her hand hovering over the checklist. "I emailed them to you a few weeks ago."

"I sure do, and we'll play anything else you want us to," Floyd added. Was he flirting with her? I suppressed a giggle and watched Christie squirm. This was definitely more fun for spectators than the dating app she was always on.

She went over the details for arrival and setup, and Floyd ensured we had everything they needed in terms of power, both at the house in case of weather, and at the dance floor near the lake.

"I've had one request from the bride," Floyd said. "It's a surprise for Jack."

"Oh? Grace didn't say anything to us." I looked to Christie for confirmation.

She shook her head. "Let me guess, a special song so she can dance for her husband with her bridesmaids? Her friend Eloise probably put her up to it. It's a real trend these days to have a flash mob, or a choreographed dance with the wedding party."

"Not exactly. Graced wanted to surprise Jack by having his uncle Rickie play a song with us. Of course, I said that would be great. I haven't seen Rickie in decades."

"Rickie? Jack's uncle, Richard? How are you connected?" Christie asked.

"Oh, we go way back. Rickie was one of the OG members of the band back in high school. Let's see, there was me, Rickie Alcott, Jed Baumann, Reggie White, and Norah Kincaid in those days. We played together for years, until Reggie quit the band and Rickie left town." Floyd grinned. "Best drummer I ever played with. Don't tell Zander. I'd love to play with Rickie again. And it'll be a cool surprise for Jack, too."

I leaned back in my chair and crossed my legs. "We don't think Richard's going to be attending the wedding, actually. He RSVP'd yes, but recently texted Jack to send his regrets. There's a little confusion about what he plans to do."

Floyd appeared genuinely disappointed. "Now that's a real shame. Would like to see the old guy again. When he left Lakewood, he never came back. Not for high school reunions, not for weddings or funerals. Moved to Toronto first, then I heard he went to Kingston. It was like he just cut himself off from all of us." Floyd's cheerful expression shifted, and I noted a hint of sadness before he rallied and grinned again. "Well, if he turns up, we'll get him to play with us."

"Since you knew him so well back then, do you think there was any reason he didn't want to come back here?"

Christie practically kicked me under the table. It was just a little mystery, but I couldn't help wondering why Richard Alcott wouldn't come to his favourite nephew's wedding, or why he'd avoided Lakewood for decades.

Floyd considered my question. "It was a long time ago. You know how it is when you're young. All kinds of nonsense and drama. I can't think of anything in particular that would drive him away, though." Floyd cleared his throat and made to stand. "Lots of young people move from small towns to the big city."

Christie stood up and shook his hand again. "Thanks for coming in. We're looking forward to the rehearsal dinner and to hearing you play. Grace says Northern Spirit is the best band in town, and the only one that covers all the oldies."

Floyd grinned. "She's got that right. We're oldies ourselves, but young at heart, as they say." He winked at Christie, and her blush deepened.

Just then, her phone pinged. I recognized it from her dating app.

"Oh hey, you're on that thing, too? Any luck?" Floyd asked, nodding towards her cell phone.

Christie crossed her arms, displaying slight defiance. "Sometimes," she said. "You?"

Floyd shook his head, his eyes twinkling. "Not really. A few good first dates, but that's all. We should compare notes sometime."

Christie walked Floyd to the front door, and I stayed in the Aurora room tapping my foot on the hardwood floor. Hugo cuddled into my lap, and Freya appeared, rubbing against my leg. I checked the windowsill for Astrid, and there she was, sunning herself in her favourite spot.

Richard Alcott had every right to skip his nephew's wedding, but there was more to it than Jack was letting on. Something had happened in Lakewood, all those years ago, to keep Richard away. If I could figure out what happened, I could convince Rick to attend the wedding and give both Grace and Jack the surprise they deserved. Meanwhile, I suspected Christie was about to have another first date.

Chapter 8

The week flew by as Christie and I prepared for the rehearsal dinner and wedding. On Thursday, I made my way to Heritage Street, stopping at Winterberry and Willow Florists. The scent of bouquets displayed in buckets outside the shop enticed me to pause and literally smell the roses. I had tucked the checklist Christie had given me into my pocket and held my phone in case there were any last-minute tasks I had to accomplish.

A customer exited the shop holding a gigantic bouquet of peonies, irises, and baby's breath.

"Someone's lucky day," I said to the young man, who grinned and nodded, but didn't chat. He was clean-shaven and dressed neatly. A birthday, perhaps, or an anniversary? I couldn't remember the last time anyone had given me flowers on a special occasion. Of course, with Mom's garden, I hardly needed a reason to receive bouquets. But still ...

He held the door open for me, and I entered Winterberry and Willow, overwhelmed by the displays of colour and multitude of bouquet choices. At a long wooden table, Lucy was wrapping flowers in cellophane, with beautiful wrapping paper hanging behind her and rows of ribbon ready to be cut.

"Hey, Minna. Christie mentioned you'd drop by today. She wanted me to organize the drop off time for tomorrow with you," Lucy said, looking up from her work. Lucy was a petite woman with long, delicate fingers and an intense stare that sometimes unnerved me, but she was one of the most creative women I'd met since moving back to Lakewood.

"You know Christie. Her list is so organized, but her time is so short. That's what I'm for."

"Oh, give yourself more credit than that. You've been working hard to get the house done up for all of your events. James has told me all about it." Lucy taped the cellophane in place and reached for a roll of white paper with tiny pastel flowers creating a looping pattern.

The mention of James made my heart leap. "Do you know James?" I wasn't jealous, just curious.

"Sure, we've been friends for ages. When James moved back to Lakewood to look after Henri a few years back, we reconnected. He's a good guy." Lucy stared at me, and I felt suddenly self-conscious.

"Yeah, he is." I held back all the questions I had about their relationship. James and I were friends, after all, but his personal life was none of my business. "Okay, let's go over the list. Mom has the garden under control, and the flower arrangements for the rehearsal dinner tomorrow. Can you drop off the boutonnieres and bouquets on Saturday by 11:00 a.m.? The ceremony is at 3:00 p.m., but they want to do some pictures beforehand."

"You got it," Lucy said. "And I have the head-table flowers, too."

"Yup, I forgot about those. I think that's it." I checked the list and accounted for all the members of the wedding party. "The shop looks amazing, by the way," I said, stifling a sneeze. I loved flowers, but my allergies weren't so appreciative. "You'll be at the wedding?"

Lucy nodded. She'd finished wrapping the bouquet and slipped a pre-written card into it. "Wouldn't miss it for the world. Nothing exciting happens in Lakewood, so it's nice to get out of the house once in a while. See you there?"

"See you there." I smiled my brightest smile. I knew for a fact James hadn't invited a plus one, so it wasn't like they were going to the wedding together. Even if they were, what was it to me?

Outside the shop, I couldn't stifle a sneeze. Or the next one. Within a space of two minutes, I must have sneezed twenty times. Time to get some allergy medication.

I crossed Pine Street, tempted to stop in at Fika and Frosting, but kept on towards the grocer's. It was a small grocery store that carried local fruit and veg, along with a host of other items, including a small pharmacy section. I searched the shelves until I found the allergy meds I needed. In the same aisle, I noticed a man squatting down in front of the pain medications, his long hair unmistakable.

"Floyd?" I asked.

He grinned. "Oh, hey. What's up, girl?"

It had been a long time since anyone had called me girl, but Floyd's easy-going nature made me feel young again. "Just trying to get a handle on my allergies before the wedding tomorrow."

"I get you. I need some headache meds before the band plays. I used to handle it, but these days my head hurts by the third song. Not that I have much hearing left," he added.

"Actually, I'm happy I bumped into you. I was really curious about Richard Alcott's involvement with the band. What did you say he played?" I hoped I sounded nonchalant about it.

"Rickie was an awesome drummer in high school. When he left, we got Zander involved, but it took him a while to level up to Rickie's standards. Damn shame he didn't keep playing. Could have gone somewhere with him, I reckon." Floyd shook his head.

"Why did Richard—Rickie—leave the band?"

"Something about a girl, I think. You know how it is. You play with the guys in your parents' garage for years, but you don't share everything that's going on. At least, when we were kids. Now, we only talk about everyone's aches and pains and surgeries." He laughed. "Rickie and I were friends, but it was all about the music. He wasn't one to share too much."

"I get it," I said. "And the rest of the band stayed intact?"

"Not exactly. Reggie split around the same time as Rickie, but came back eventually. Worked out west. He joins us once in a while, likes to keep up with his music, but doesn't want to commit to playing too much. Has a partner now who he spends time with instead of being out on the road."

"That makes sense," I said. "See you at the rehearsal dinner. I'm looking forward to meeting the rest of the band."

Floyd gave me a salute and turned back to the drugs on the shelf. If he had any other knowledge about Richard, he wasn't sharing, but it seemed to me he was honest about what he knew. And that wasn't much.

Chapter 9

"Welcome to Hygge House," Christie said, ushering in Grace's maid of honour, Eloise Lockheart.

Eloise was shorter than she looked in her social media posts, but every hair was in place and her makeup looked like a professional had done it. Despite being in her early thirties, she presented as a much younger woman, very aware of her appearance. I guess you'd have to be self-conscious if you were always posting on social media.

"How was your flight?" I asked. Eloise had flown from Paris to Toronto before transferring to our local airport. The trip sounded exhausting, but the thought of Paris was alluring.

"Delightful. There's nothing like a good travel video for my fans. They're always excited about where I'm going next. I only wish I could have been here for the bridal shower, but I was at an event in London."

Eloise barely took a breath when she spoke, as if she needed to get everything out at once before someone stopped her. She glanced around the foyer. "It's darling. I can't wait to capture the essence of this town. It's been so long since I've been back. I grew up here, but my parents moved to Muskoka a few years after I left for Paris. And you've simply transformed this old place. Plus, the wedding—it's going to be spectacular."

Christie's expression must have given judgmental vibes because Eloise paused. "Oh, don't get me wrong. This trip is all about Grace and her wedding. I'm always in work mode, though. Can't help but see everything as a beautiful shot or moment to capture. It's what I do, you know. Occupational hazard."

"No judgment from me," I said. "Snap away." I glanced around for her luggage, noticing only her expensive designer bag. Sofia was going to drool over it. "You travel light. Do you have any other bags?"

"Light?" Eloise laughed. "No, my luggage is in the Uber. Do you mind?"

I did mind, but I smiled and shrugged when Christie gave me *the look.*

"I'll take care of them for you, Ms. Lockheart. I'll deliver them right up to your room." I should have felt humiliated by catering to this woman, but she fascinated me. Everything about her life was the polar opposite to what I wanted to create for myself here in Lakewood, and yet we'd grown up in the same small town.

"Oh, call me Eloise. Everyone does. What a quaint place you have here. I'd love a tour. Do you mind if I take photos? Some videos for my Insta?" Eloise fluttered her long eyelashes and tilted her head.

"Of course," Christie said. "I'll introduce you to Sofia, who does our social media. You have a lot in common."

"Does she have 1.6 million followers, too?" Eloise's face practically lit up from the inside. Her dewy glow was nearly electric.

"I'm afraid not. We've just been in business for a few months," I said, "but we're working on it." How could one person have that many followers? I'd need to check out her feed to see what it was all about.

Eloise waved her hand. "No problem. By the time the weekend is done, we'll have that account buzzing with followers. Just wait and see." Eloise posed by the staircase and stared at the stained-glass windows. "Grace mentioned that she's hired a local band. When are they arriving?"

"They'll set up as we're having dinner, and then there will be time to enjoy their playing in the evening," Christie said. She led Eloise up the grand staircase, pausing as she took photos and stopped to take a selfie from the top of the stairs, looking down on the foyer and the stained glass windows she'd admired.

I headed toward the Uber. The driver was already lifting Eloise's many suitcases out of the trunk.

"Thanks so much for waiting," I said, reaching for the rolling suitcase and carry-on.

"You're welcome. Have fun with selfie-girl," he said before getting in his car and driving away.

I couldn't help but chuckle. She might be selfie-girl, but with that many social media followers, she could get our business a little attention. It surprised me that Eloise was Grace's maid of honour, but apparently they'd been friends since childhood, just like me and Christie. One could never tell, really. What you saw on the surface wasn't really who someone was inside. Just like posts on social media were only a version of reality.

As I pulled the luggage toward the stairs—thank goodness for bags with wheels—James drove up in his truck, hopped out, and took them from my hands.

"I can handle them," I said. I was still feeling weak, but overall I was much better. Good thing, too.

"I know you can, but you should rest," he said. "Where to?"

"Room 3," I replied, grateful for his attention. "We really need proper names for the rooms. Fanny's room will always be Fanny's room, but numbered rooms feel too cold."

A car pulled up and parked in the visitor's spot.

"Your timing is perfect, actually. Looks like Lillian Alcott is back with her family."

Out of the dark sedan, Lillian Alcott appeared from the passenger seat. Little Rosie hopped out of the car and raced to the porch, where Hugo Dogberg covered her in licks. A tall, handsome man accompanied Kate. He must be Jack's older brother, Ian.

"Welcome to Hygge House," I said. "So happy to see you again." This time, everyone carried their own luggage. No influencers here, apparently.

"Oh, Minna," Lillian said. "It's been quite a day. I can't wait to sit in front of your lovely fireplace with a glass of wine."

"That can be arranged," I said, smiling. She really was a woman after my heart.

The keys were ready, tucked into cute envelopes with some information about the wedding events and the local area. They'd already received the schedule Sofia had designed, along with hand-drawn maps of the area.

I handed Kate her family's envelope, and she thanked me. "Let's drop off our stuff and take a walk on the boardwalk," she said to her husband. "You'll love this town."

"Great idea," Ian said, giving his wife a shoulder squeeze.

"Yeah, Daddy," Rosie said, clapping her hands together. "Let's go for a walk."

I gave them directions to their room and wished them a pleasant stroll. Lillian took her envelope, but instead of heading up the stairs, she paused, as if ready to share a secret.

"I have some good news," Lillian said, her voice a dramatic stage whisper. "Richard will attend the wedding after all! I'm so pleased."

"Really? I hadn't heard. What made him change his mind?" I asked. Thank goodness we had kept his room at Driftwood Cottages, or the man would have had nowhere to stay tonight.

Lillian beamed with satisfaction. "I called him and told him not coming to the wedding was affecting Jack and his big day. I was very persuasive. It was enough to change his mind."

"Jack's going to be thrilled, and Grace will be so relieved. Good for you," I added. I imagined Lillian was the type of person who could put the pressure on. She was hard to say no to. "Did Richard say why he hadn't wanted to come?"

Lillian shrugged and picked up a light bag, leaving the heavier one for James to transport. "The man's a mystery. Let's just be happy he's on his way."

As Lillian plodded up the stairs, Christie bounced down them.

"That Eloise Lockheart is something else," Christie whispered. "This wedding is going to make social media history, if she has anything to say about it. She took pictures of everything: the view, the bed, the pillows ... even the lampshade."

I grinned and shoved her arm. "Don't get too excited about it. It's not likely that her followers will flock to Lakewood soon. Oh, and Richard Alcott is on his way. Lillian has convinced her brother-in-law to show up after all."

Christie pulled out her phone. "Well done, Lillian. I'll text Driftwood Cottages to confirm his reservation. Everything is falling into place now. I hope."

"Aren't you pleased with that news?" I studied Christie's face, concentrating as she texted.

"In my experience, anyone who causes issues before an event is bound to cause bigger issues at the event. Mark my words, Richard Alcott is about to make trouble."

"From everything I've heard, he sounds perfectly fine. I'm sure you're exaggerating," I said, trying to lighten the mood. But Christie was rarely wrong about these things. She'd organized so many events in the past twenty years or more, and she'd seen everything.

"I hope you're right on this one," Christie said.

"Me too," I said. "Our guests are here, except for the bride and groom. Let the celebrations begin."

Chapter 10

James was chopping wood for the bonfire, ready to be lit after the rehearsal dinner. By then the sun would set, and it would be a perfect time to celebrate Midsummer and the upcoming wedding. I could already imagine how beautiful the fire would look with the lake as its backdrop.

"It's ready to go," James said, striding up the path toward me, looking a little like a lumberjack in his t-shirt, jeans, and work boots. "To tell you the truth, this is the first time I've made such an enormous bonfire. Should have warned the fire department."

"I wouldn't worry about it. The fire's so close to the lake, and there are no fire bans this season. At least, not yet."

Although Grace had no Scandinavian roots, she loved the idea of celebrating her nuptials on the longest day of the year, and of course, Christie and I embraced the idea, suggesting Nordic traditions at every turn. The Nordic countries marked Midsummer with dancing and bonfires to celebrate the upcoming harvest. It made for a great wedding theme and perfect timing.

I grinned. "Just wait until you see it. Midsummer Eve has always been a magical time in our family," I said, explaining how my father would create a big fire by the lake and friends would gather around, singing, drinking, and dancing as the sun lowered and the flames licked the sky. Mom had told me stories about White Nights during her childhood in Finland—months when the sun barely set—and the myths surrounding Midsummer about love and fertility, and how bonfires warded off evil spirits and flowers held special powers.

"Sounds amazing. I'm looking forward t my first Midsummer celebration. Anything else I can do to help?" James asked, brushing his hands on his jeans.

I pictured Christie's checklist as we headed toward the house. The chairs were being set up for the ceremony, and the tables were set. "No, I think everything's under control for once." I hesitated. "Lucy said she'd be at the wedding. You two are friends, I take it?"

James's eyes widened. Was he blushing? "Lucy Chen? Yeah, we've known each other for years. We were in a lot of classes together in high school."

"Hmm. Did you date?" I asked, feeling a little bold. I didn't want to pry into his life, but I also wanted to know about the connection between Lucy and James.

"We did, but we're just friends now."

"I see," I said, hoping I didn't sound jealous. Lucy was a beautiful woman and ran a successful business. A catch for any bachelor in town, my mother would say. Could Lucy have been James's elusive fiancée?

"Right. I'll go home and get changed and be back after the rehearsal dinner to light it up. Just text if you need me."

Time to get my head in the game. In about three hours, Grace and Jack would arrive, along with their wedding party and special guests. I was confident, mostly, that everything would go off without a hitch, no pun intended.

James ambled across the lawn toward the front of the house, and I couldn't help but watch him go, still wondering whether he and Lucy Chen were more than just friends.

At 3:00 p.m., the family gathered in the garden, where we'd already set up the wedding arch covered in vines and flowers, and the chairs in neat rows with floral bows attached to the backs.

I shook hands with Pastor Fredrick Dahl, the same man who led Owen Bradshaw's funeral service. He was a lovely man, rotund and red-faced, with a good-humoured nature and an easy laugh. I could see why Grace wanted him to officiate.

"The big day is almost here, Minna," Pastor Dahl said. "Are the stars ready?" He asked, scanning the small crowd milling around the chairs.

I glanced at my phone to check the time.

"I'll see if they're inside." I found Lillian chatting with my mother. The two women had become fast friends, it seemed, in just a short time.

"We're the same vintage," my mother had said when I'd asked her. "Or nearly. I'm a little older and wiser. But don't tell her I said so. She likes to hold court."

Christie was in the kitchen with Grace and Jack. "The pastor is asking for you," I said, not wanting to interrupt, but conscious of the time.

Jack nodded, but didn't smile. Grace gave me a pleading look. "We were holding off for Uncle Rick, but he's not here yet. Good thing the groom made it on time. Can you believe he and Harry went to play pool this afternoon?"

"Just wanted to blow off some steam," Jack said. "Besides, I'm not the one who's late." He pulled out his phone, probably checking if his uncle had sent him any texts. He frowned.

"What if we started, and he joins us when he gets here?" I suggested.

Christie nodded and headed towards the door, motioning for the couple to follow her. "He could be behind schedule. Highway traffic can be terrible on a Friday, with everyone heading out of Toronto to their cottages and all the tourists flocking in for the weekend. The main thing is he shows up for the wedding, right?"

"Yeah, let's do this. Hopefully, he'll make it here for dinner." Jack's voice betrayed his disappointment. He turned to his bride-to-be and attempted a smile. "Let's not keep everyone waiting. We have some rehearsing to do."

Grace returned his gesture with a wide smile and a squeeze of his hand. Christie and I followed them through the breakfast nook and watched from the sidelines as the wedding party organized themselves and the minister gave instructions. The rehearsal was seamless, and the bride appeared relaxed and relieved. Even Eloise was on her best behaviour, only snapping a few photos while they rehearsed and one selfie with the wedding guests in the background.

After the rehearsal, we ushered the wedding party into the renovated sunroom, with its long harvest table decorated with twinkle lights, a linen tablecloth, and flowers from our garden.

"You've outdone yourselves," Lillian said as she entered the space. It was positively glowing in the warm light, and was both sophisticated and natural at the same time. The perfect hygge vibe. "I must say, I wasn't sure about having the wedding here when Jack and Grace told me about it. Not after hearing about Grace's brother and ... well, everything. But I understand it now. You are lovely hosts, and this place is so elegant."

"Thank you, Lillian," Christie said, showing her to her seat. I directed Kate and Ian to their places, and seated Rosie between Kate and Eloise. The maid of honour and the flower girl had really hit it off, and Rosie wanted her photo taken at every turn.

Once the bridesmaid, Priya, and the best man, Harry, along with Pastor Dahl, had taken their seats, the table was full. Almost. Only one seat remained—Uncle Rick's. I moved to take away his place setting, but Jack stopped my hand. "Let's leave it, in case he joins us later."

I nodded and stepped back. Jack checked his cellphone for the umpteenth time that day, but apparently there were no messages from his uncle. He shoved his phone into his jacket pocket.

Grace positively glowed in the candlelight, happier than I'd seen her in the several weeks leading up to the event. She'd had so many difficult moments in the past few months. She deserved this moment. Eloise stood up and manoeuvred around the table, nudging guests to move over as she got the perfect shots of the place settings, the flower arrangement, the wine glasses, and the bride and groom-to-be.

Not to be outdone by our carefully prepared decor, Michael Holmes and his servers arrived with platters of food for the occasion. Dressed in black shirts and pants, along with pinstripe aprons, the staff looked professional and well-trained. Michael had opted for a smorgasbord with a variety of hot and cold dishes, including pickled herring, smoked salmon, devilled eggs, Swedish meatballs, new baby potatoes with fresh dill, rye and crispbread, and pickled beets. The guests dug in as if they hadn't had a good meal in days.

Christie and I exited the sunroom, allowing the attendees some private time to talk and eat. Grace had invited us to take part in the dinner, but we'd declined, although we'd agreed to be guests, as well as hosts, on the wedding day itself.

"It's going great, right?" Christie whispered to me in the hall. She looked pleased, but her nervous energy was clear.

I nodded, trying to feel enthusiastic, but something was nagging at me. "Yeah, everything's perfect."

"What's wrong? What aren't you telling me?" Christie pulled me by the arm away from our guests.

I sighed and suggested we get some fresh air, away from the kitchen and sunroom, in case someone might overhear us. Hugo Dogberg bounded downstairs as we opened the front door, happy to be in the company of his people once more.

"I find it strange that Richard said he was coming to the rehearsal dinner, but hasn't contacted Jack all day. If he were simply running late, wouldn't he just send a quick text?"

"Yeah, you're right," Christie said.

We strolled around the circular driveway, past the visitor parking area. I recognized Ian and Kate's vehicle, and Jack's SUV. The pastor drove a two-seater electric car that I always wondered how he could squeeze himself into, but admired his eco-friendly choice.

As we approached, I glanced at the side of the house, where Christie and I parked beside Michael's Lakewood Catering van, its doors wide open.

"Wait. Whose car is that?" I asked.

"No idea. Someone from Michael's catering staff?"

"Let's check it out."

Christie and I reached the car. I peered through the window, but there was no one inside. Thank goodness. I tried the door, but it was locked, of course.

"Do you think it's his?" Christie asked, cupping her eyes and leaning down to search through the backseat window.

"I can't imagine whose car it could be." I leaned against the car and crossed my arms.

"We could check with Michael and his staff," Christie suggested.

"Good idea. If it doesn't belong to a guest or someone from the catering staff, I have an idea."

"Oh, no. You're going to leave me, aren't you?"

"Listen, you have everything under control. James will be on his way soon to light the fire. After the meal, Michael will serve coffee and dessert, and then they'll head outside for the bonfire. The band will play for a while. Mom's here if you need help."

"You have a scheme up your sleeve," Christie said. "What are you going to do?"

"Nothing. I mean, I'm just going to go over to Driftwood Cottages and see if Richard has checked in, make sure everything's okay. If he drove all this way to Lakewood, and even came to the house, why hasn't anyone seen him? You check the house and I'll check the cottage."

"Let me save you some time." Christie pulled out her phone and texted Driftwood Cottages. A few seconds later, she received confirmation. Richard Alcott had checked in during the early afternoon.

"Okay, that's good news, I think. I'll head over and see if he's still there. If all is well, I'll drive him back for the bonfire and surprise Jack. If he's not okay, I'll handle it. There could be a medical emergency or something."

Christie shook her head. "This doesn't make sense. If this is his car, why would he go back to the cottage without it? There has to be another explanation."

I agreed. "A good reason for me to check it out, right? I won't be long, and I'll text you when I learn more. And Christie? Be discreet about asking whose car this is until we get more details."

"Got it," Christie said. "Be careful. I'll text you about what I find here."

I smiled and nodded as if I went looking for missing guests all the time. "Don't worry. It's not like I'm investigating a murder or anything. Just checking on our guest. Maybe I'll bring Hugo. He'll protect me."

Christie raised an eyebrow. "Hugo might lick a criminal's face off, but I wouldn't trust him to protect you from anyone. Leave him here with me. Just don't be foolish, okay?"

I nearly laughed aloud. If anyone was apt to get themselves into some trouble, it would have to be Christie. "Don't worry. I'll be back soon."

Chapter 11

Driftwood Cottages was a sprawling resort west of the historic downtown. I drove along Lakeshore Drive, past the pier and Heritage Street, and continued along the winding road toward the property. As I got further from town, the houses were farther apart, cottages replacing the historic brick buildings, and with an occasional modern build imposing itself on the otherwise idyllic landscape.

When Christie and I were teens, the place was pretty rundown, and some locals lived there full-time despite its lack of insulation and proper heating. They had a good beach where tourists and locals alike gathered. I remembered my mother warning us about swimming out too far. A young woman's body had been found one summer. Drowned and dragged by the undertow. I shivered at the memory.

Since I'd left Lakewood, the resort had been purchased, and the cottages renovated so they could be rented in all seasons. Now, they were a popular place to stay, especially for outdoorsy people who wanted to take advantage of summer water sports like swimming, kayaking, and fishing, and winter ones like cross-country skiing and snowmobiling.

I parked in the visitor lot and locked my door, not that I was worried about anything, but old habits from the big city die hard. The main lodge housed a restaurant, a bar, a pool table, and a library with a cozy fireplace. Christie and I had had lunch here one afternoon, just to check it out before we booked rooms for our guests.

No one was at reception when I arrived, so I waited patiently, eyeing the front desk for any clues. Most hotels kept their registries on computer programs, but Driftwood Cottages was old school. They had big, clunky keys attached to decorative pieces of driftwood hanging behind the registration desk. On the desk, I noticed the date book open with guests' names and cottage numbers, neatly handwritten in calligraphy. A Schaeffer pen sat in the spine of the open book. I struggled to read it upside down, but I wished my handwriting was as legible.

"Can I help you?" A middle-aged woman appeared from a back room, wiping her mouth. I'd probably interrupted her during her dinner break. She had raven-black hair and big dark eyes, with lipstick that looked out of the 1940s. Her name tag, slightly crooked and well-worn, said, 'Stella, Guest Services Representative.'

"Sorry to interrupt," I said. "I'm Minna Halonen, from over at Hygge House. My business partner, Christie Andersson, has been dealing with the reservations here for the wedding guests."

Stella nodded. She popped a piece of gum into her mouth and chewed. "Okay."

I hesitated. "Has Richard Alcott checked in?" I glanced at the day planner and back at Stella.

"Yes, he checked in." Stella crossed her arms as if daring me to ask more questions. For a guest services representative, she didn't have the guest services part down.

"Can you tell me which cottage he's in?" I had to ask, but I could tell by her face that she wasn't playing.

"As you are well aware, that's confidential information," Stella said, raising an eyebrow.

"Yes, of course. It's just, we expected him at Hygge House and he didn't arrive." I fumbled as I spoke. Did Stella think I was incompetent at running my business? "I thought ... as colleagues ..."

"Nope. Can't help you," Stella said before I could finish. She picked up her pen and focussed on the guest book, a clear sign she wasn't answering any more of my questions.

"Can you call his room?"

Stella sighed and rang the number. I could hear it ringing, but no answer.

"Can you leave him a message? Ask him to call me at this number?" I wrote my cell number and passed it to Stella, who reluctantly took it. I thanked her and wished her a good evening, breathing with relief when I exited the lodge. The heat on my face and body was momentarily relieved by the cool air. Hot flashes come at the most inopportune times, usually when I am trying to be professional.

Heading toward my car, I noticed the recently posted signs leading to the various cottages. Stella wouldn't tell me the name of his cottage, but the number beside his name in the registry was fourteen. The sign pointing toward Cottage 14 included the name Crow's Nest.

In keeping with the atmosphere of the area, there was no lighting along the trails to lead me. I pulled out my cellphone and clicked on the flashlight, hoping I'd have enough battery power to get me there and back. The wooded trail wound past several cottages, some lit from within, one with an external porch light on, and a few unlit. Crow's Nest was at the end of the path, perched on a rocky hill overlooking the lake. The view must be stunning from the cottage.

The porch light was dark, and so was the interior. If Richard were here, he could be asleep and have missed the rehearsal altogether. The car didn't belong to our guests or to the staff. If it was Richard's car, why would it be at Hygge House if he was still here? Glancing around the cottage, I saw nothing unusual—not that I expected to see broken glass or a banged-in door, but it was better to be cautious.

Three steps led up to the porch and the front door. I knocked and waited. I knocked again. No response. I closed my eyes and pictured the day planner, reading Richard Alcott's name upside down and the cottage number. Definitely fourteen, and not nineteen or seventeen. I was confident this was his room, even if the guest representative, Stella, would not confirm it.

If Detective Christopher Whitford were here, he'd tell me to go home. It was no business of mine whether Jack's uncle wanted to attend the rehearsal or not. I paused with my hand on the doorknob. "You might be right, Whitford, but what if you're not?" My voice was a whisper, but it was comforting to hear a sound that wasn't straight out of the *Blair Witch Project.*

I turned the knob. Locked. So, I did what any self-respecting amateur sleuth would do: I tried all the windows and the sliding door from the patio, but to no avail. I had one more trick up my sleeve. To be honest, I'd never actually tried it before, but I'd seen it work on plenty of murder mystery series. I pulled a bobby pin from my hair and grabbed a credit card from my cellphone case.

I slid the credit card into the gap between the door and the doorframe until I got to the latch, wiggling it while leaning into the door. I tried the doorknob. No luck. I didn't know what the bobby pin was for, so I tucked it into my pocket. The amateur sleuths on television made it look so easy.

A sound in the bush nearby made me pause. What if someone saw me trying to break into the cottage? No one appeared, and I figured it must have been a squirrel or chipmunk. Hopefully nothing larger, like a bear. Taking a deep breath, I tried again. This time, I felt the lock move, and as I turned the knob, the door swung open. Success.

The front door led straight into a living room area with a couch, two armchairs, a coffee table, and a fireplace. Double doors led out to a covered porch overlooking Long Lake, where pine trees rustled against the exterior logs and birch trees swayed near the water.

From the living area, I made my way across the room to the small but fully functional kitchen. Two glasses sat on the rustic kitchen table beside an opened bottle of whisky. One looked untouched, half full, at least, while the other was empty, with only a few drops at the bottom. Who else had been here with Rick and had a drink?

Summoning my courage, I called his name. If Richard were here and had hurt himself, or fallen asleep, the last thing I wanted was to scare him to death by showing up beside him. We hadn't even met yet.

The long corridor from the living room to the back of the cottage had two doors on the left, one on the right, and a fourth at the end of the hall. I knocked on the first door and waited. No response. The door creaked as I opened it. No one was there.

Driving up to Driftwood Cottages, I hadn't felt nervous about checking for Richard—more curious than anything else—but now, in the dim cottage in the dark woods, with very few people to hear me if I screamed, my anxiety grew. Steadying my breath, I stepped toward the door and opened it. Another bedroom. Empty and untouched. Across the hall, a third door opened to a luxurious bathroom with a large tub and a window overlooking the woods. A toothbrush sat on the side of the sink, along with a tube of partially used toothpaste. Someone had been here.

The last door stood before me, barring me from what lay inside. What would I find? Richard Alcott sleeping? Injured? Dead? I pushed the thought aside. Ever since Owen Bradshaw's death on the doorstep of Hygge House, my imagination had a tendency to spin out of control.

Another deep breath and I turned the knob, directing the light onto the floor at first, not wanting to shine it into his face if he were there. I raised my cellphone and moved the light across the room.

"Richard? Rick Alcott? Are you here?" I asked, trying to sound pleasant, but my voice was wavering.

On the bed, someone had laid out a grey suit with a shirt and tie, ready to be worn to the rehearsal dinner. In the closet, a black suit, a white shirt, and navy tie, with dress shoes to match. Richard had been careful to unpack his clothes for the wedding. But where was he?

On the bedside table, I found the schedule for Grace and Jack's wedding, the one Sofia had designed for their special occasion, along with the map insert of the town and attractions, including directions to Hygge House. Richard had grown up in Lakewood and would have remembered the layout of the town. There was no reason he couldn't find the place.

What else was I looking for? What clues would tell me where Richard Alcott was? I didn't know what I was looking for, so I controlled my breathing and scanned the room again, slowly taking in all the details. My memory would hold what I saw until I needed the details. It was my superpower. At least, that's what I liked to think. Deep down, I hoped Richard Alcott had just gone for a walk on Mosquito Trail, perhaps up to Misty Veil Falls, and missed the celebrations. It's possible he'd gotten lost.

I closed the door behind me and paused on the deck to text Christie about Richard's absence. Someone had stubbed out their cigarette on the railing. I checked the ground near the stairs. Another cigarette butt with red lipstick stains, and a third had been crushed underfoot. Had Richard met a woman here? Richard must be somewhere in Lakewood. We just needed to find him before the wedding.

As I pulled out of the resort's parking area and down the narrow road toward Lakeshore Drive, a truck skidded down the road at a high speed, enough to make me want to blare my horn. I restrained myself. It was likely one of their guests who was unfamiliar with the dark and windy roads. Luckily, I had just enough space to pull to the side before his high beams nearly blinded me.

What a night. I couldn't wait to tuck into my bed and get some sleep before Saturday's event.

By the time I returned to Hygge House, our guests were gathered around the bonfire with drinks in hand. The band was playing, and some guests sang along to "Singing on the Dock of the Bay." Appropriate, since they were literally on a dock on a bay, singing their hearts out and swaying to music.

I found James adding some logs to the fire, even though it was large enough that someone might call the fire department on us.

"There you are," he said, his face lit by the flames. "Christie told me what you were up to. Any news?"

I shook my head and stared across the fire at the bride and groom, Jack twirling Grace around as they danced and sang. Even Lillian appeared to be relaxed, dancing with Rosie standing on the tops of her feet.

"He wasn't in the cottage," I said, trying not to attract attention. I caught Christie's eye, and she excused herself from chatting with Kate and picked her way around the bonfire to where I stood with James.

"No text from you, so I'm guessing it's bad news," Christie said, her eyebrows furrowed.

"Not exactly. He definitely checked in and had clothes laid out for the rehearsal dinner, I'm assuming, and his suit was hanging in the closet, ready for the ceremony tomorrow. But I saw no sign of him anywhere."

"Did they give you a key?" Christie crossed her arms and leaned towards me.

"No key. The receptionist was less than helpful."

"Ah, you met Stella. She's all business and no fun," Christie said. "Not sure she likes her job. How did you get in?"

"I ... well, I guess I could say I let myself in," I said, conscious now that I had basically broken into the cottage and snooped around. At least I didn't steal anything.

James emitted a low whistle. "That was risky, even for Nancy Drew. Good thing no one caught you."

"What about the car? Did you figure out who owns it?"

Christie shook her head. "It doesn't belong to any of the staff or the guests. It's a mystery."

"Yeah, but now I don't know whether I should tell Jack or wait until morning. What if Richard decided against coming to the rehearsal, but intends to come to the wedding tomorrow? It could have been a conscious choice." I tried to sound reasonable. "He's a grown adult, after all."

Christie stared at the still lake, and I turned to it, too, watching the flames reflect off the still, dark water and dance towards the night sky, already dotted with stars. James used a long pole to poke at the fire, causing sparks to fly.

Christie broke the silence. "I agree. Let's wait until tomorrow. The man has every right to make his own decisions."

I glanced at James, wanting his opinion. So often, he was the voice of reason. "James?"

He shook his head. "You two need to decide what's best. But if you don't find him by tomorrow, you need to come clean with the groom."

Christie and I reached for each other's hands and squeezed. He was right, and we both knew it.

Chapter 12

The morning of the wedding flew by. Eloise was working on Grace's hair and makeup, while Lillian, Kate, and Priya waited their turns, chatting about the day's events. Jack, Ian, and Harry had gone out for a men's breakfast at the nearest greasy spoon in Birchwood, although we'd offered them a full breakfast at Hygge House.

When the doorbell rang, I sprang into action, leaving the women to their preparations. "Oh, thank goodness you're here," I said, opening the front door to Lucy Chen. In her arms, she carried a large, flat box with no top, revealing carefully laid out boutonnieres. "The flowers are so beautiful. Can I take them from you?"

"Yes, please. There's more in the car," Lucy said.

"Right. I'll take these upstairs to the bridal suite and come down to help you." I glanced at my phone. Christie had stepped out but promised to be back soon. I hoped everything was okay. It was a big day. Not only for the bride and groom but also for our business.

As Lucy returned carrying the bouquets, another car drove up and parked in the circular driveway. Tyler Shore appeared, dressed neatly in dress pants, a collared shirt, and a tie, carrying an impressive camera. Sofia had convinced Grace that Tyler was a talented photographer who could offer low rates since he was just building his portfolio. We'd admired his samples, many of them featuring Sofia and other locals. He had a gift; that was for sure. Could Eloise have met her match?

"The bride is upstairs, Tyler," I said, directing him to the bridal suite. As he scampered up the stairs, my mother walked carefully down, pausing on the landing to stare at me.

"What am I looking for?" she asked, a puzzled expression crossing her face.

"I don't know, Mom. What are you looking for?" I thought of my mother as being very sharp, especially for her age, but lately these kinds of questions were happening more often.

Lucy followed Tyler up the stairs, careful not to crush the bouquets.

"Silly me," she said. "I'll have a cup of coffee and some breakfast. I'm sure it will come to me." She toddled off toward the kitchen, where Michael was already setting up for the day. Terri had outdone herself again, delivering the wedding cake earlier that morning. Everything was ticking along nicely.

I glanced at the time again. Where could Christie be? But before I could text her, her car rolled into the parking lot, and she jogged toward me, a dressing bag held high in her hands.

"What's this all about?" I asked. "You forgot your dress?"

Christie blushed. "No, I forgot Grace's gown. I promised to pick it up yesterday from Annabelle's and completely neglected to put it on the checklist. Amateur mistake."

Lucy appeared and smirked at Christie. "Forgot the dress again?"

"You got me," Christie said. "But it only happened one other time, and that wasn't really my fault. My assistant was supposed to get the dress and forgot to tell me she got delayed."

The expression of dismay on Christie's face made me laugh out loud. "If that's the worst that happens today, we're going to have an amazing event. Plus, the bride isn't quite ready for the gown yet, anyway. Eloise is putting the finishing touches on her hair and makeup."

"Thank goodness," Christie said. "Is it safe to go up there?"

"I think so. They look adorable, all dressed in matching silk pajamas, slippers, and robes with their roles embroidered. Tyler's going to get some great pre-wedding shots."

"We really appreciate you delivering the wedding flowers. Apparently, picking up orders is not Christie's strength," I said.

"No worries. I've got your back, Minna," Lucy said. "See you at the ceremony."

As Lucy pulled away, Christie turned to me. "In my defence, I make a great checklist."

"Indeed. And no one needs to know you almost forgot the dress."

Christie sighed and headed up the stairs to the bridal suite. My phone rang, and I picked it up, heading into Taiga Hall, where we'd already set up for the dinner. "James? What's up?" I asked.

"Just wanted to tell you I've checked in with the hospital and the police. I combed the trails and made some inquiries in town. No one has seen Richard Alcott," he said.

"Thanks, James. You didn't have to do all that, but I'm glad you did," I said. The knot in my stomach clenched, and I reminded myself to breathe.

"You need to tell him, Minna. Jack needs to understand that Richard is missing." James's voice was serious.

"You're right. I'll tell him as soon as he gets back," I said. "If anyone should tell Grace, it should be Jack." I hung up the phone and called for Hugo, who dutifully sprang to my side. "Come on, boy. Let's get a short walk in before the day gets any crazier." Hugo's tail wagged furiously as I put on his halter and leash.

Instead of the trails, we headed towards the garden, so I could take one last look at the setup for the ceremony. We wandered to the lakeshore, where the bandstand was ready for the musicians and the platform James had created was waiting for dancers. There was enough time for a quick walk down the boardwalk, but I couldn't help but scan every male face wondering if they were Richard Alcott, as though he might have a stroll along the lake as if it were any other Saturday morning, and not the day of his favourite nephew's wedding.

Chapter 13

"Nope, I don't want to hear it," Jack said, raising his hand up to my face. "I've been so frustrated with Uncle Rick over the past few weeks, and it's affected Grace. Not today." Jack pushed past me on the verandah and opened the front door to Hygge House. His best man, Harry, followed behind, shrugging as he passed me.

"Jack, hear me out," I said, not wanting to alarm him, but feeling a duty to tell him his uncle was missing.

"If Uncle Rick wants to come to the wedding, he will be here. If he doesn't want to come, let him. I'm done worrying about it." Jack stomped into the house and up the stairs, with Harry at his heels. That left me on my own, wondering what to do next.

"Right. Decision made. On with the day," I said to no one in particular. Hugo plopped himself on the verandah, his head in his paws, looking at me with sad puppy-dog eyes.

"What are you looking at?" I asked. One of his ears popped up, and he raised his eyebrows. "Okay, I know. I'll tell him, but I'll wait until I know more. Besides, Rick might just show up at any moment." Hugo covered his eyes with a paw. "I feel you, buddy. I want to hide sometimes, too."

The rest of the day flew by as we made final preparations, primped the bows, and adjusted flowers, ensuring everything was perfect.

By the time the ceremony was about to begin, I was exhausted, but also happy, and a little nervous.

Christie grabbed my hand and squeezed it. "It's going great," she said in her enthusiastic and reassuring voice. "Stop worrying."

"How did you know I was concerned?" I said, smiling at a guest who passed us to take a seat in the audience.

Christie laughed. "You wear your heart on your sleeve. One glance at you, and I can tell how you're feeling. You'd make a terrible poker player." Christie wasn't wrong. I couldn't help but absorb other people's emotions. I must be picking up on Grace's excitement and nervousness, because I'd already done my job and there was nothing left but to watch the ceremony.

Christie and I seated ourselves in the back row, with James beside me on my left. Mom looked as beautiful as the mother of the bride, and Henri appeared proudly in his updated suit. Sophia and Tyler sat to Christie's right, looking the picture of youth. To my relief, Lucy Chen sat a few rows ahead of us with a dis-tinguished-looking gentleman. Was he her date? Not someone I recognized, but I cringed at my earlier reaction to her relationship with James. Of course, there was no reason I should be jealous of Lucy. James and I were just friends.

The string quartet started playing John Legend's "All of Me." Rosie walked down the garden path toward the aisle flanked by wedding guests, scattering rose petals and stealing the show, as children often do.

"What a darling girl," my mother said, her tissue already in her hand.

After Rosie, Priya strolled arm-in-arm with Ian, smiling at the guests as they passed. Then came Eloise and Harry. Eloise was stunning, and she knew it, while Harry looked a little hungover.

"I'm impressed. Eloise doesn't even have her phone in her hand," I whispered to Christie.

"Think again. She has it tucked away in her dress. Look closely."

Indeed, Christie was right. Eloise had her phone. With any luck, she had it on mute. I sighed. At least Tyler was using a proper camera to capture the ceremony. I glanced around and found him taking shots of the bride as she began her journey from the house to the bridal arch where her groom awaited.

As the music changed to the "Bridal Chorus," guests stood up and turned to see Grace. She radiated joy and confidence. Michael Holmes had agreed to walk her up the aisle, and it made sense to me. With no father to walk her, her boss, Michael, was someone she could rely on, and his pride in being at her side was clear as he guided her. I may have detected a tear or two.

"She looks stunning," Christie whispered as Grace came into view. I agreed, allowing myself to relax for the first time that day. Everything was going as planned.

I caught Annabelle's eye on the other side of the aisle. She was beaming with pride at her creation; the Midsummer wreath was the crowning achievement. The guests gasped with delight, and I overheard several comments about her glorious gown.

Jack waited for his bride, looking more relaxed than we'd seen him earlier. He'd said he wanted the perfect day, and he would not let his upset about Uncle Rick ruin it for him. He was right after all, but I still scanned the crowd for Richard.

Pastor Dahl delivered a charming ceremony, and the guests' laughter tinkled through the garden. Like magic. Vows spoken, rings given and received, kisses exchanged, and applause abounded.

No one had forgotten the rings. The weather had held. There were no blackflies or mosquitoes to speak of. Only no Uncle Rick had arrived. I pushed away the thought and focussed on the happy couple as they took photographs in the garden. Between Tyler's photos and Eloise's videos and selfies, Grace and Jack would have many memories preserved of this day.

"We did it, kid," Christie said, giving me a quick hug, a glass of champagne held away from my dress in one hand. When she released me, her smile faded. "Why the long face?"

"Remember how I was going to tell Jack about his uncle? He wouldn't let me say a thing. He refused to hear any bad news." The guilt was eating at me, but how could I deny Jack's wishes on his wedding day?

"That is *not* your fault. You tried. Let them enjoy the event. Besides, I'm sure Richard will contact them when he's ready." Christie didn't look entirely convinced, but Sally and Betty waved her over to the drinks table. She touched my arm and turned on her charming host persona to join them.

The rest of the day went smoothly. We served dinner in Taiga Hall, Michael having insisted on serving indoors so as not to attract any flies and just in case the weather turned. I saw his point, but an outdoor dinner would have been lovely if we'd ordered tents. Next time.

After the cutting of the cake and dessert, Grace and Jack led the guests to the outdoor dance floor where Northern Spirit started playing. Fairy lights strung above the dance floor illuminated the space as the sun slowly set, painting the sky in pinks, purples, and golds. After a few minutes, Harry and Eloise joined them, along with Ian and Priya, and then the other guests, forming partners to dance under the emerging stars. I watched Henri weave through the dancers to ask my mother to dance. They looked great together.

James took my hand and led me without a word to the dance floor. We fell into each other's arms as if we'd been dancing together all our lives, the most natural thing in the world. I let my worries seep away.

There was nothing to worry about. The wedding was a success. Grace and Jack were happy, and the guests were enjoying themselves. I let my head lean against James's shoulder, feeling his hand on my lower back and my fingers in his, allowing myself to feel a little of the magic we'd created.

Chapter 14

A few hours later, exhausted but feeling good, I sat beside Christie by the firepit as James let the flames die down.

"Thanks for a great evening," Priya said. "Grace is so happy, and the wedding was perfect. The two of you did outstanding work. You must be so relieved."

Christie beamed and gave Priya a big hug. "You have no idea. Thanks for the lovely compliment. Have time for a drink?"

Priya shook her head. "I'm exhausted, and I'm not sure I can handle any more selfies with Eloise." We glanced at the maid of honour, who was posing with the members of the band, her arm around Norah, changing her phone angles at every turn. She'd already captured every view of the house, the garden, and the lake, and spent hours capturing every detail of the wedding itself.

I laughed out loud. "Well, maybe her social media posts will get us some new guests. It could become the top attraction in Lakewood." As irritated as I was about Eloise constantly being on her phone, I secretly hoped the attention on Hygge House would give us a much-needed boost. Owen's murder earlier in the spring didn't help our reputation, despite the curious visitors and those interested in ghost stories.

"You'd be surprised at what Eloise's touch can do to a place. After she's sprinkled her fairy dust, a whole town's economy can grow. I've seen it happen," Priya said. "It's pretty amazing."

"Was she always like this at school?" I asked, glancing at Eloise, who was giving Norah a hug as if they'd been long-time friends.

Priya laughed. "You mean, attention seeking? She has always been the star of the show. Star of the school plays, sang in every choir, and danced her little heart out. She loves the attention, but she's also the sweetest person ever."

"Hmm," I said. "She seems to have a big heart. I love how she's taken care of Rosie this whole time, and quietly helped Grace get ready without pressuring her. She has a gentle touch."

"That's Eloise for sure. She lives a big life, but she cares deeply about people. I think it's because she grew up without knowing who her biological parents were. Her adoptive parents made sure she had everything. Maybe they were a little over-generous, but they taught her to be a good person." Priya smiled and said goodnight.

I watched her stroll across the lawn, past the bandstand, and join Harry, who had been lingering nearby with Dev. My mother had already toddled off to bed hours earlier, but Tyler and Sofia were still going strong.

The band packed up, playing some slow jazz on the speakers for the last few couples as they put away their instruments and dismantled their mics, speakers, and cords. Northern Spirit had been a complete success, keeping dancers of all ages moving on the dance floor all evening.

"I almost forgot. I have a cheque for Floyd and the group," Christie said, reaching into her pocket. "Got to love a dress with pockets."

I followed Christie to the bandstand. She went straight to Floyd with their payment. Norah was just wrapping her mic cord.

"Thanks so much, Norah." I said. "You have a lovely voice, and the band sounded so great. We were all impressed."

She stepped off the bandstand and took a seat on the edge of the stage, taking a drink from her water bottle. "Great venue. I love what you've done with this old place. I remember driving my bike up the boardwalk as a kid and wondering who lived here, thinking they must have been straight out of the nineteenth century."

"Same here. I always thought it was a grand old house but kinda sad, too. Needed some real TLC." I gazed up at the house, the windows glowing from the interior lights, and sighed. Sometimes homes not only have a history but a spirit—not just like Fanny's ghost—but a personality. Renovating her was like uncovering that spirit again.

Norah took another sip of water. "I hope you'll think of us in the future for your events. Most of us don't want to tour much anymore. Not as young as we used to be. But events in town are so convenient."

"Of course," I replied. "Christie has your contact information. She does all the bookings. I'm sure she'll recommend you to future wedding parties and other events."

"Too bad Rickie Alcott didn't make it. I was looking forward to playing with him again. It's been probably thirty years or more. More like forty." She shook her head. "Time passes so quickly."

Good thing the lights were dim, or she might have noticed the concern I was trying to hide. "Yes, it would have been great to hear him play, and I'm sure the groom would have wanted him here. Sometimes things happen, I guess."

Christie was on the bandstand chatting with Floyd and passed him the cheque. Just like last time, he turned on his charm. The man was probably quite persuasive in his day, but I didn't imagine Christie would fall for him. Not that he was much older than her—less than a decade—but he wasn't her usual type.

Jed placed his guitar in its case and stopped to thank me and say goodnight to Norah. "Got to check on the kids," he said.

"Drop by the kitchen. Michael will give you some cake to take home to them," I suggested. I knew there was so much left over, and Jed's kids would be thrilled.

"So your band has been together since high school?" I asked, returning my attention to Norah.

"Pretty much. Not always the same musicians, but that's what happens with bands. People come and go."

"Any reason Rick wouldn't want to attend Jack and Grace's wedding, do you think?" I didn't want to start rumours, but the message Richard had sent Jack was pretty clear. He didn't want to disturb the past. What wasn't clear was what had happened then that made him want to stay away.

Norah shook her head. "No, I don't think so." She turned abruptly and grabbed her bag and coat. "Thanks again, Minna. We had a great night." Before I knew it, she was waving goodbye to her bandmates and striding across the lawn to the visitor parking. Eloise watched her leave. It seemed selfie-girl was the singer's fangirl.

"What did you say to Norah?" Christie asked, stepping down the stairs, concern written on her face. "She looked a little upset."

"Not much. I asked her about Richard, but she had nothing to say." I shrugged. "Let's go see if James needs any help."

We joined James by the firepit, where he was enjoying the glow from the embers and a cold drink.

"Okay, that's it for me. It was a fun night," he said. "And the rehearsal dinner was superb, too. My first Midsummer with a proper Scandinavian bonfire, and I think I did okay. Didn't burn anything down." James chuckled as he raked the glowing embers. "Tonight's firepit is more my speed, though."

"Both events were just perfect. Just how we envisioned them. My mother just glowed when she spoke about the bonfire. She couldn't stop talking about her youth in Finland. I think the wedding party and guests thought it was pretty cool, too."

"Any news about Jack's uncle?" James asked.

I shook my head. "I'm still worried. He didn't show up for today's ceremony or the reception. And his car is still here on the property." I hoped Jack would be more receptive the following day.

Christie and I sat on Muskoka chairs, finishing our drinks. I took off my high heels and wiggled my toes, stretching my legs out.

"We did it," Christie said. "Our very first wedding was a complete success." She raised her hand, and we gave each other a high-five like we'd done as kids.

"I guess we could get a start on the cleanup," I suggested, looking around at the debris left behind, including streamers, and flowers, and wine glasses.

"Nope. Let's leave it until the morning," Christie said. Her decision sounded so definitive; who was I to argue?

I agreed, but I picked up the empty glasses and plates, along with some napkins left behind on the chairs and benches near the firepit. Christie followed me, picking up items as she went. A little farther, past the firepit and the far end of the dock, I paused. Something caught my attention, but I couldn't quite make it out.

"What's that?" I said, pointing. Could it be an animal? It wasn't moving, but the light was too dim to see any details.

Christie pulled her cellphone out of her dress pocket and flashed a light in that direction. The closer we got, the clearer it became. A lone Muskoka chair sat facing the lakeside, but it wasn't empty.

A man sat in the chair, his arms flung to the sides and head rolled back. Was it a guest taking a break from the festivities? Consumed too much and needed to rest? Fallen asleep?

Christie grabbed my arm, and we approached him, careful not to startle him if he was sleeping. I reached out my hand and touched his arm. He didn't respond.

"Hello? Are you okay?" I asked, but there was no reply. A momentary flash of Owen Bradshaw sprawled out on the breakfast nook floor made me freeze. I shook off the dread that had gathered in the pit of my belly. Based on the man's age and appearance, he could have some kind of medical issue.

"Call emergency," I said, but Christie was already dialing.

I could barely hear her explaining the situation to the dispatcher, but my focus was on the man in front of me. I didn't recall seeing him at the ceremony or at the dinner. If this were a guest, he'd have made himself scarce. But he might not be part of the wedding. Many tourists and locals took strolls on the boardwalk at all times of day and night. He may have needed a rest and saw the Muskoka chair positioned with a view of the lake.

Unless ... could it be Richard Alcott? He was wearing light trousers and a polo shirt, along with runners, not attire one would expect for a wedding guest. No one had seen Richard today or at the rehearsal dinner yesterday. Could he have come for the rehearsal and ended up here, taking in the view until the event started, wanting to surprise everyone? My imagination wove in all different directions as I stared at the man, looking for signs of injury or death. I checked his pulse and his breathing. I spoke loudly and gently shook him.

"They're on the way," Christie said, returning to my side. "Is he dead?"

"Yes, I think so." There were no visible signs of life or foul play. Judging from his frame, the man was overweight. His face was ruddy in the way drinkers' faces often are, and his fingers were slightly yellowed. An overweight smoker who drank too much.

"He could have had a heart attack," I said.

Christie let out a long breath. "Yeah, it's probably natural causes. If he were struggling, he may have sat here to catch his breath or relax. An asthma attack or a stroke, perhaps. Lise Tremblay will figure out what happened to the poor guy."

"You don't think it could be—"

"Richard Alcott?" Christie interjected. "I really hope not."

From a distance, we could hear the ambulance and police vehicles coming down the lane toward Hygge House. The party had only just ended, and although the guests had left, the family and wedding party were in the house. Surely, they would wonder what happened and be out here soon, too.

"I think one of us should go to the house. I'm guessing the guests are going to have questions," I said.

Christie nodded. "Do you want to draw straws to see who stays with the body?" Christie had a strong distaste for blood and death.

"I'll stay. You go on up and let them know what we've found. But don't mention Richard just yet." There was no reason to alarm the family, especially if it turned out this was just a local or tourist out for a walk. If it were Richard Alcott, we'd know soon enough.

Christie trudged back to the house, disappearing into the dark shadows before her figure reappeared under the lights near the house. She spoke to the officers and pointed towards where I waited by the waterfront. I took the last few minutes to search the area with the light from my cellphone. Nothing unusual. Only a napkin from the house in pale pink near the chair, the same kind we used at the rehearsal dinner. How did it get here? Tonight's choice was white linen for the wedding. If it were daylight, I'd see more, but for now, I'd have to let the police take over.

The ambulance attendants checked the man's vitals and confirmed his death, speaking in hushed tones to Detective Whitford. I stood back from the scene, reluctant to leave in case they needed me, hoping I could learn something about this stranger.

"Minna Halonen, I see you have a penchant for finding dead bodies," Detective Whitford said, strolling toward me. "Hygge House is getting quite the reputation around the police station, I might add."

"You're joking, right?" I asked.

Whitford didn't answer. "Any idea who this is?"

"I'm not sure, but it could be Richard Alcott, the groom's uncle. We expected him yesterday, and we think his car is here, but no one has seen him." If there were more light, Whitford would surely see my red face. I should have reported him missing on Friday, and here we were, in the very early morning hours of Sunday, and the man might be dead. Could I have prevented this?

"Okay. We'll have Jack Alcott confirm his identity," Whitford said. "But not here. He'll meet us at the coroner's office." I understood Whitford needed to follow procedure. It was better for Jack to identify his uncle there, if this was, in fact, Richard Alcott.

Before Detective Whitford could explain anything else, someone came racing down the lawn. Jack, still in his dress pants and his shirt unbuttoned, ran barefoot towards us, with Grace a close second, still in her white gown, her hair undone and looking wild.

Officer Roxanne Grey stepped in front and told him to stop, trying to restrain him from approaching the body, but Jack struggled. Whitford gave Officer Grey a nod, and she let Jack go.

"Is it him? Is it Uncle Rick?" Jack asked, now holding himself back from the sight of the dead man. It was one thing to want to know, and quite another to have to see.

"We don't know," I said, my voice gentle. Jack's eyes were wild, and he raised a fist to his mouth. "Why don't you go to the house? The police will ask you to identify him at the coroner's office."

Jack shook his head. "No. No. I need to see." He crept forward. Grace stood back, hugging her torso. What a terrible way for their fairytale night to end.

I stepped away and let Jack take my place, close enough to see the body clearly. Whitford used his flashlight to light the man's face. Jack covered his mouth.

"Can you identify him?" Detective Whitford asked. He was uncomfortable at that moment. This wasn't following protocol. I admired his professionalism paired with compassion for Jack, but I knew Whitford didn't like this one bit.

Jack nodded. "It's him. It's my Uncle Rick. Richard Alcott."

From the knoll, Grace let out a cry, and my heart sank.

Chapter 15

C hristie shook her head. "Are you crazy? We can't just waltz into Driftwood and check out a dead man's cottage."

The police were still investigating on our property, looking for any signs of wrongdoing. It was late, or perhaps it was early; I couldn't tell anymore. "If we don't go now, the police will get there before us, and we'll never find out what really happened." I grabbed Christie's hand and dragged her across the lawn where Sofia and my mother huddled together, wrapped in blankets.

"Mom, Christie and I have something we need to do. Can you deal with the police and the guests?"

My mother eyed me suspiciously. "Really? Now?"

I nodded and hoped she could read in my eyes my unsaid pleas. I couldn't tell her anything, or the police might ask her where we were, and she'd have to tell them. "We'll be back before they're done here. I promise."

Mom gave a curt nod and wrapped her arm around Sofia's waist. "Loose lips sink ships," she said, and I knew she'd stay silent. She probably even knew where we were going, but no one would pull out her suspicions. She'd never lie outright, but lies of omission, well, that was something else.

Christie and I trod through the house and out the side door. "Better not take the car. They'll definitely stop us."

"You're right. I'll text James to meet us at the end of the park." It was too far to walk to Driftwood Cottages and get back in a decent time. James would help. I was sure of it.

We headed towards the forest trail, unlit at this time of night, but as soon as we were a little way down the trail, I turned on the flashlight on my phone. My battery was running low, but I could practically walk this trail by heart. This time, I wished I had Hugo Dogberg with me, not that he was much of a guard dog, but still. Reports of foxes in the area made me a little nervous. Of course, they were probably more afraid of me than I was of them. Worse, reports of bears in the woods made me walk faster and talk a little louder.

"Do we have a plan?" Christie asked, her strides matching mine. If our middle-aged bodies had been up to it, we'd jog, but a fast walk was the best we could do.

"James will drive us to the cottages. We'll take a quick look and get out of there as fast as we can."

"Are you looking for anything in particular?" Christie asked, sounding breathless.

"Not exactly. I'll know it when I see it," I said. How could I explain that something was off in my visual memory of the room? I needed to see it again. There was something missing.

A set of headlights nearly blinded me as we headed into the parking lot. I jumped into the passenger seat and Christie into the backseat.

"Ladies, where to?" James asked, stifling a yawn. Even decked in a flannel shirt and old jeans, clearly having just woken up, he was still cute.

"Driftwood Cottages," I said. "And make it quick." In my head, I sounded like some detective from a hard-boiled mystery straight out of the 1930s. I drew in a breath, trying to channel my inner Miss Marple. She never seemed to get shaken.

"Should I ask?" James glanced into his rearview mirror at Christie.

"I wouldn't," Christie said. I glanced back, too, and she had her arms crossed.

"Please drive us to Driftwood Cottages. We'll take it from there," I said, this time in a calmer voice.

"Are you going to fill me in?" James navigated out of the parking lot and down the hill towards Lakeshore Drive.

As he drove, I told him everything that had happened since he'd left the wedding.

James let out a low whistle as he pulled into Driftwood's visitor parking. He opened his driver's side door.

"Whoa? What do you think you're doing?" I asked.

"Coming with you?" It sounded more like a question than an answer.

"Nope. You stay here with the truck. We may need a getaway car. You up for that?" The last thing I needed was for James to get into trouble on my behalf. If I was going to do it, I would do it alone. Well, I was okay with taking Christie down with me. That was always our gig.

"You got it, Nancy Drew," he said. "But if you're not back soon, I'm coming in. Do you want me to stay in the parking lot?"

"Might be better if you park on the road a little ways down, just in case the police arrive," I said, trying to sound casual. "We'll go through the wooded area and find you on the road. I'll flash my light to let you know where we are."

"Got it," James said. "And Minna?" Even in the dim light, I could make out the concern on his face. "Be careful. Don't take any unnecessary chances."

"Got it," I said, jumping out of the truck and closing the door behind me.

Christie and I slunk away from the truck and headed toward Crow's Nest. It was probably for the best that the trails weren't properly lit as we skulked our way down the path. This time, I didn't even turn on the flashlight on my cellphone. Besides, it was better if I preserved the battery. And at least there was no evidence of a police presence. Yet.

"How are we going to get in?" Christie asked, her voice a barely audible whisper.

I held up my credit card.

"We're going to rent a room?"

"Follow me." We climbed the stairs, and I used my credit card trick to open the lock. At least this time it worked right away, unlike last time. I was getting better at this. Meanwhile, Christie kept an eye out, nearly jumping out of her skin when an owl hooted nearby.

"Are you sure about this?" I could barely make out Christie's features, but her eyes were wide. "Isn't this breaking and entering?"

"Good question, but I'm going in." This time I turned on my cellphone's flashlight. "You keep an eye out and signal me if anyone is coming."

When we were kids, we had a signal that involved a whistle that sounded like a bird. I didn't need to remind her what to do.

Christie nodded. She seemed relieved not to enter, although there was no evidence that it was a crime scene; it was surely a place of interest to the police. And to me.

Using the same path I used last time, I entered the living room. It looked exactly as I'd left it. I was careful not to touch anything. In the kitchen, I remembered the glasses and the whiskey bottle. Someone had a drink with Richard. One glass was empty. The other was half full. No lipstick stains, I noted.

I strode down the hall, remembering the two bedrooms on the left and the bathroom on the right, but I headed straight to the back to Richard's room. There were the clothes he was probably planning to wear to the rehearsal dinner. And the suit for the wedding. On the bedside table, I paused. The wedding schedule was exactly where it had been earlier. The directions to Hygge House were missing. In its place was a note on Driftwood Cottages's stationery, written in tidy handwriting.

I squatted beside the bedside table and shone my flashlight on the note. It hadn't been there earlier. I knew that as a fact. This wasn't a reminder or a scrawled phone number. This was a note addressed to Lillian. I read it aloud, committing it to memory.

Dearest Lillian,

I'm sorry it has to end this way. In time, I hope you will forgive me for what I've done.

All my love,

Rick

Was it a suicide note? When had he placed it here? After I came to Crow's Nest looking for him? Or did someone else place it here? Was it even his handwriting? I set my phone camera to night light and took a photograph of the letter, careful not to touch it. Lillian might have insight into what it meant.

"Minna," Christie whispered as I approached the front door. "I saw flashing lights approaching. The police are on their way."

My heart beat faster, and I clicked the thumb lock from the inside. "You'd think the resort would have changed the locks to something more secure. These old locks are probably original to the resort. Anyone can just break in," I said, shutting the door and checking that it locked after me.

Christie used her sleeve to wipe the doorknob. "What? I'm trying to get rid of your fingerprints."

"Good call," I said. We snuck back onto the trail, and then behind a dark cottage. I tried to still my breathing as we heard officers moving toward the cottage, their flashlights in hand. When they were safely inside, we ran through the bush, past the parking lot, and towards James's truck.

"I've never been so relieved to see someone," I said, climbing into his truck.

"Good thing you came. I was about to come and get you. I saw the police pulling up and tried texting you, but there was no answer."

"Aw, you were worried about me," I said, trying to tease him, but his concern was clear on his furrowed brow and the tension around his mouth.

"In fact, I was worried. Good thing you had your sidekick with you." James turned on the ignition and inched away, his lights off until we cleared the property.

Christie swatted him and smiled. "Yeah, good thing. If she goes to jail, so do I. Am I taking you with us as an accomplice?" We all laughed, but it was more uncomfortable sounding than I'd hoped. This time, I may have taken it too far. Just because I could break in didn't mean I should. Even I knew I'd crossed a line. But I had seen Richard's note, and that gave me pause.

Chapter 16

A few short hours later, after a troubled sleep, our guests gathered in the Stuga room, haggard from their own sleeplessness. We laid out a table with food and coffee, but no one moved to eat. We were all in shock, and nothing I could think to say would make it better.

"Coffee, Lillian?" Mom asked, delivering her a cup and saucer, which Lillian accepted but did not drink. "A terrible tragedy." It was a relief to have my mother with us, saying the right things. It wasn't the first time she'd comforted someone after the death of a family member.

Dark circles framed the haunted expression in Lillian's eyes. "I just can't believe he's gone. And I'm the one who convinced him to come here. I practically begged him." She stared at my mother with fear crossing her face.

Mom sat beside her and took her hand in both of hers. "It's not your fault, Lillian."

"We don't know what happened yet," I added. "There's no reason to blame yourself."

I delivered coffee to Kate and Ian, who sat on the loveseat. Kate's downcast expression revealed her sadness, and Ian's expression was one of shock. Only Rosie had any energy, and she was playing with Hugo Dogberg outside where we could see them through the window, unaware of the tragedy that had befallen their family. Astrid was sitting in her usual spot on the window seat, watching as Rosie threw the ball and Hugo retrieved it. I imagined she had disdain for their activity and for the human emotions weighing on the room.

"Uncle Rick didn't say why he didn't want to come to the wedding, did he?" Ian directed his question to Jack.

Jack shifted uncomfortably where he stood near the fireplace and ran his fingers through his tousled hair. He was still in the pants and white shirt he'd worn for his wedding. "He must have had his reasons, but he didn't share them with me. His text said, 'Better for me not to disturb the past.' What does that even mean?"

Grace huddled in the couch's corner, her feet tucked into her chest, looking more forlorn than I'd seen her since she'd lost her brother. Eloise sat beside her, one arm around her shoulder. I wove my way through the furniture and knelt beside her. "You okay? You look like you could use some fresh air."

Grace attempted a smile. "I'm not feeling very well, but I'll be okay. It's been a lot, you know?"

"Let me get you something to eat." I picked up a plate and placed a few pieces of pulla—Finnish coffee bread—and some berries on it before delivering it to Grace.

When everyone had been served, I poured myself a cup of coffee and observed the family, each in their own world, but together in unified support.

"I hate to mention it, but did Richard have any health concerns?" I asked, remembering Richard's corpse.

Lillian sighed. "I told him he needed to stop smoking, and that drinking would not do any good for his heart."

"He had a heart problem?" Jack asked, his eyes widening.

"Yes, of course. He had the same issue your father had," Lillian said. "And until now, he had been managing it. Only lately, he'd been getting into bad habits. Gained weight, started drinking more. I warned him, but he was so stubborn." Lillian shook her head and wiped the tears forming in her eyes.

Christie appeared at the door. "Minna and I would like to offer an extension of your stay—on us, of course. The coroner should have answers soon."

"That's so kind of you," Grace said.

"Mom, are you okay here a little longer? You're welcome to stay at our apartment, but space is tight." Jack leaned towards his mother.

"No, Jack. I'm perfectly comfortable here. Thank you, Christie and Minna. I just can't leave until I understand what happened." Lillian stifled a sob and dabbed her eyes with a handkerchief.

Ian took out his phone and started texting. When Kate nudged him, he said, "What? Just letting my boss know I need a few more days." She seemed satisfied with that answer and leaned her head on her husband's shoulder.

"I'm afraid I can't change my flight, but I'm here for a few days more. I'll do anything I can to help," Eloise said, directing her attention to Grace.

Christie crossed her arms. "Well, the first thing you should do is avoid posting any photos or videos connected to the death. We don't need your fans speculating about what happened here."

Eloise's eyes widened, and she nodded. "Yes, of course. I'll be very selective. Besides, a social media break is always a good idea. I'll tell my followers I'm taking a hiatus." Eloise took out her phone and started typing with her long, perfectly manicured fingernails. "Done."

"That's settled then," I said. "Please tell us how we can help you over the next few days."

The family nodded and thanked us. Christie and I headed to the garden, where we had a party to clean up after. The sight of it made me want to crawl back into bed, but I didn't want to leave any evidence of the wedding aftermath. The grieving family had enough to worry about.

After a few hours, we had everything in place again. The rental company came to pick up the chairs and tables we'd rented and drove away. All that remained was the wedding arch, still adorned with flowers and ribbons. I didn't have the heart to remove it just yet.

"Any theories?" Christie asked as we headed toward the house, Hugo Dogberg following close behind. Kate and Ian had taken Rosie to the local park for a while, leaving Lillian to rest in her room.

"Truthfully? I think he had a heart attack or some other health crisis. Lillian mentioned he wasn't a healthy man."

"Um, okay." Christie said, giving me the side-eye.

"What does that mean?" I paused on the path and crossed my arms.

"It means you always have a theory. And it's never something as simple as a heart attack. You must be considering all the options," Christie said.

"Nope. No theories. I'm waiting to hear from the coroner. Lise will tell us what happened. Until then, it's just conjecture." I was determined to keep my suspicions to myself. I didn't want to concern the family any further.

"Right," Christie said, nodding. "So you do have some theories, but you're not telling me."

"What about you? How do *you* think he died?" I asked, curious about Christie's thinking.

"Why would a man check in, drive his car to the event location, and go by himself in his everyday clothes to the lake and sit on a Muskoka chair? If he were coming to the rehearsal, wouldn't he have worn the clothes he laid out for himself? And he had a suit for the wedding, ready to go. I don't buy it. He didn't just happen to die at our lakefront." Christie crossed her arms and leaned in, egging me on.

I shrugged and smiled. "We'll see." This time, I would let the police take care of it. Detective Whitford didn't want me involved in any investigations, and that was fine with me. "Let's focus on the business and taking care of our guests, not on searching for a murderer. Besides, there is no evidence of foul play, so there's that." I turned toward the house and strolled up the path, lugging a garbage bag to the side of the house.

"Okay," Christie said. "Let's make the family as comfortable as possible while they're here. You're right and I'm wrong."

I laughed. I wasn't so sure about that, but time would tell. And Christie knew me well enough to understand I couldn't let this mystery go unsolved, even if his death was from natural causes. But I wasn't ready to tell anyone about the note I'd found, the note that suggested Richard had taken his own life. For now, I'd wait to hear what the police had to say about it. And Lillian.

Chapter 17

Christie and I ordered our lattes and took a seat by the window. Boreal Beanery was quiet this morning, with only a few regulars dropping in for their standard orders. The tourist season had ramped up, despite our reservations about traffic after Owen Bradshaw's murder earlier in the spring. I hoped this fresh case wouldn't deter them, too.

"Anything else?" Sarah asked a few minutes later, dropping our mugs off at the table. "I have some lovely blueberry scones if the mood strikes you."

I loved Sarah's Aussie accent and her kind nature. "Sounds yummy, but I have no appetite," I said, trying not to sound like a downer.

"You doin' okay? I heard about the wedding and the dead uncle. Oh, sorry. That wasn't very sensitive of me," Sarah said.

Christie shrugged. "The whole town has heard by now." Ever since Richard Alcott's death, Christie had fallen into a slump. It was so unlike her usual cheerful nature. It worried me. We had everything riding on this business, and a second death on the property could be the end of it all.

"I haven't lived here as long as the two of you, but this town is always looking for a bit of gossip. Don't let it worry you. And Christie once told me if there was a problem to be solved, Minna could solve it." Sarah glanced at me with a twinkle in her eye.

"Yeah, thanks for that, Christie. But I shouldn't get involved in this one. Whitford has given me explicit instructions to stay out of Lakewood's crimes."

"And you're going to listen to him?" Christie asked. "Since when do you take anyone's instructions?" She knew me better than anyone, and she was right. I had to admit, as soon as someone told me what to do, my instinct was to do the opposite. Maybe that was part of my Finnish DNA.

I gave Christie a light punch on the arm and took a sip of the latte. "Mmm. So good. I'll have one of those scones now," I said, hoping to change the subject. In fact, I could barely think about anything else but Richard's death and the apparent suicide note.

Sarah touched my shoulder and strode toward the counter where her husband, Brian, was arranging freshly baked goods in the display case. "Two blueberry scones," she said, calling out to him.

Brian looked up and gave us two thumbs up. "G'day, ladies. Coming right up."

A few minutes later, after enjoying our lattes and scones, Christie broke the silence. "What are you thinking?"

"I'm not thinking anything," I said, watching a couple across the street pausing before entering a shop.

Christie raised an eyebrow. "Is that even possible in that head of yours?"

"I'm thinking I need to speak to Lillian. She knows more about her brother-in-law than she's letting on. Look," I said, handing her my cellphone with the image of the note I'd taken on the night of the break-in.

"Is this from Crow's Nest?" Christie zoomed in on the image, her eyes widening as she read the note. "Have the police seen this?"

"I would assume so. They arrived right after I took this picture. Don't you think it's strange that Richard left a note addressed to Lillian of all people? Sure, they were relatives, but it still seems off to me. And I swear the note wasn't there the first time I broke in—I mean, went to visit Richard."

"Someone planted the note?" Christie returned my phone.

"Could be." In truth, I could have missed it, but it wasn't like me not to remember details. Menopausal brain fog was a real thing, though, and I could have forgotten it, or not even noticed it. Or Richard wrote it after I'd broken in. I had too many questions. "I need to find out what Lillian's relationship was like with Richard and why he's so apologetic to her."

Christie brightened up. "So, you're on the case? I knew it."

"Looks like it. But don't tell anyone," I said, putting my cell-phone back in my purse. It was good to see Christie's face animate again, as if she were slowly coming back to life.

"Mum's the word," she said, beaming. "You couldn't resist, and now we can solve this case and redeem ourselves. No one can blame us for the murders happening at Hygge House if we're the ones who solve them."

I agreed. It was about Hygge House, but it was also about Jack and Grace. They'd already gone through too much. They needed justice, and I was going to make sure they got it.

Chapter 18

A few hours later, exhausted from the recent events, I wandered outside with Hugo Dogberg, breathing in the fresh air. Lillian sat on the garden bench by the wedding arch. Despite her pensive mood, it made for the perfect photograph, but it seemed inappropriate to take a photo of her just now. Not after everything she'd endured.

As I approached, Lillian's expression lightened, and she smiled. Like my mother, she could hide her emotions. "Oh, Minna. Are you looking for me?" There was a hopefulness in her eyes that saddened me. We hadn't heard from the coroner's office or the police. Waiting was becoming difficult for everyone.

"Just needed to get outside," I said. "Do you need anything, Lillian? I could get you some coffee or tea."

"No, darling. I'm just fine. Like you, I needed the air. And this spot here in the garden is so peaceful. You've created a fairy-tale garden here."

I chuckled. "I won't take credit for the garden. It's my mother's magical touch that brings it to life. May I?" I asked, nodding toward the space on the bench.

Lillian nodded, and I sat beside her. Hugo scampered through the garden, chasing butterflies. For several moments, we sat in silence, the warm sun on our skin, and a light breeze wafting past us.

"Lillian, I have something to ask you, but I'm not really sure if this is the right time," I said, breaking our silence as gently as possible.

"Darling, if there's something I've learned in my years, it's that there is never a right time. I've been wondering when you'd bring it up."

"You heard? About the note?" Hugo Dogberg bounded across the lawn, wagging his tail, demanding pats. He hopped onto my lap, and I stroked his ears.

"Of course. Richard addressed the note to me after all. That lovely Detective Whitford shared it with me when he interviewed me at the police station." Lillian didn't appear to be distraught over the note or the interview with the police.

"I see," I said, not sure how to proceed. "Why would Richard address his note to you? It seemed very personal."

Lillian paused, reaching over to scratch Hugo under the chin. "This is not common knowledge, Minna, but I'll tell you now that he's gone. We were together for decades. We didn't advertise the fact. Jack was young, and we didn't want to confuse him. We kept it a secret. For years. We didn't find the right time ..."

I was astounded. Rick and Lillian had a relationship for decades? And kept it quiet. How was that even possible? "Your relationship started after Patrick's death? Jack was only little then."

"Eleven. When Jack's father died, Richard was living in Toronto. He left his whole life there to be closer to us in Kingston, to help me with Jack, he said, but that's when our relationship started. I was the older woman." Lillian's smile appeared tinged with sadness.

Hugo jumped from my lap to chase after a butterfly, bounding through the garden, while I considered what Lillian had revealed. "You mean you fell in love?" Was I pushing her too far? To my surprise, Lillian seemed open about the secrets she'd kept all those years.

Lillian gazed into the middle distance, lost in her own thoughts. "I loved him. I have always loved him. But Rick was younger than I was. He was only a kid when we met. I married Patrick and then had the kids. After Patrick died, everything changed." Lillian wiped tears from her eyes and turned toward me. "I was free. And happy for the first time in years. I never meant for this to happen. I never told the kids. They adored their father. I was afraid they would never forgive me."

"Richard asked you to forgive him for what he'd done. What did he mean?" I asked, thinking back to the note he'd left for her.

Lillian shrugged and crossed her arms. "I suppose it has something to do with how we left it. I urged him to come and said Jack would be heartbroken about his decision, that I'd never forgive him." Lillian stifled a sob. "If I had just let it alone, he'd still be alive."

I nodded and touched her hand, giving it a gentle squeeze. "It's not your fault. What he was worried about? Why didn't he want to come here?"

"Richard could be a very private man. He was good to me, but I always felt like he had secrets. I was so angry with him about the wedding that I cut off communication. I think he wanted to surprise me by showing up at the rehearsal dinner. But—"

"I'm so sorry for your loss," I said. "Will you tell Jack now?" I asked. If this were a family secret, I didn't be the one to reveal it.

Lillian sighed and nodded her head. "I suppose I'll have to tell him. The police already know. And now you. I should tell the family myself before they find out from someone else." She stood up and straightened her blouse. "They would have been so angry about our relationship then—like I was betraying their father—but they're older. Better now than never," she said, standing tall. Without another glance my way, she strode toward the house. I admired the strength of this woman and her determination to set things right. If she were Finnish, I'd say she had *sisu*.

I whistled for Hugo Dogberg, and we headed towards Mosquito Trail. Lillian would need time for the family to digest this news, and I wanted to give them privacy. As we walked under the tall trees, I listened to the birds chirping and the needles under my feet, breathing deeply to calm my nerves. Something was still nagging at me.

The note left to Lillian sounded like a goodbye, but it hadn't explained why he didn't want to attend the wedding in Lakewood. And why would he have ended his life on Midsummer Eve during the wedding weekend? He loved Jack and was in a long-term relationship with Jack's mother, Lillian. It made little sense that he would ruin the event and have the couple start their marriage under such a dark cloud. I shook off the thought and focussed on the trail ahead. One step in front of the other, I reminded myself. That's how we get to our destination. The problem was that I didn't know where I was headed.

Chapter 19

Several days passed as the family waited for news from the coroner's office. The house felt solemn, like it too was grieving. Footsteps landed heavily on the hardwood floors throughout the house, and the creak in the stairs was more pronounced. I wanted to ask Lillian if she'd told the family, but it was not my place, so I held back.

As I washed the dishes after the morning's breakfast, I wondered how long the family would have to wait to hear the news. This should have been Jack and Grace's honeymoon, but they needed confirmation about his beloved uncle. It just didn't seem fair after all the tragedy they'd already faced in their lives.

"Need any help?" Sofia asked, sauntering into the kitchen. At least she was a beam of sunlight on this grey day.

I tossed her a fresh tea towel. "Aren't you supposed to be working at the store today?" Sofia's full-time schedule at the store, plus her social media side hustle, kept her very busy.

"Not today. Mummu said she wanted to be in the store and I could do whatever I wanted with the time." Sofia glanced around, but we were alone in the kitchen. "She needed to get out of the house," Sofia whispered.

I nodded. "I get it. It's pretty gloomy around here right now. What are your plans?"

"Tyler and I are going up to Floyd's place later today. The band is rehearsing in the garage, and they said Tyler could play with them whenever he wanted. And Norah said I could sing backup." Sofia laughed. "She might change her mind when she hears me."

"That sounds fun. Text me the address, please. Just in case." Sofia was an adult—fully baked, as she'd said when she turned twenty-five—but I still worried about her. At least she would be with Tyler. The two of them made a good pair.

Sofia rolled her eyes, but texted me anyway. Ever since Owen Bradshaw's death, she hadn't argued with me about safety protocols, even though Lakewood was probably the quietest and safest place she'd ever lived.

When the dishes were done, Sofia left to meet with Tyler, leaving me alone in the big old house. Normally, I loved being solitary, dreaming of the next renovation, but this week was different. And I wasn't actually by myself. Jack's family was scattered throughout the house, finding their own ways to cope.

The breakfast nook door creaked open, and I nearly jumped out of my skin, but it was only Christie coming in through the back way.

"You scared the wits out of me."

"Sorry about that, but I didn't want to disturb them." She nodded her chin up to a vague spot on the ceiling.

"We should plan something nice for the family. Do you think they'd like a boat ride? I could ask James to take them on the lake." I glanced outside. If only the sun would make an appearance, everyone would feel better.

"That's a good idea."

Christie's phone pinged.

"Got another date?" I asked, only half teasing, while I poured myself more coffee.

"No, it's Detective Whitford. He's on his way here. He wants us to gather the family." Christie's face paled, and her hands trembled. "He must have news about Richard Alcott."

"Let's put everyone in the Aurora Room. I'll make more coffee and tea. They may need some sustenance when they hear the news."

"I'll call Grace and tell her to bring Jack over now." Christie texted as she moved toward the back stairs and headed up toward the guest rooms.

By the time the coffee and tea were brewed, Officer Christopher Whitford was at the doorstep, along with Lise Tremblay. I held open the heavy wood door, searching their faces for any clues about what they might tell us, but both of their expressions remained neutral. Total professionals.

"Detective Whitford, Lise," I said, closing the door behind him. "The family is waiting for you in the Aurora Room. Jack and Grace are on their way."

"I'm sorry you are going through this again," Detective Whitford said, taking off his hat and holding it with both hands. "It's highly unusual to have one, let alone two—"

"Murders?" I whispered, glancing from Whitford to Lise.

Lise shook her head and raised an eyebrow.

"Now, Minna. I didn't say that. I meant two deaths in the same house, so close together." Detective Whitford shifted from foot to foot. "Shall we?"

"Yes, of course." I led them into the Aurora Room, where Lillian sat on the couch watching Rosie play outside with Hugo. Ian and Kate sat in the chairs opposite the couch, both looking uncomfortable and a little uptight.

I offered everyone tea and coffee, suddenly wishing my mother were here. She was so good in these situations. Christie passed around biscuits and pulla, along with napkins, and placed them on the coffee table before saying she'd wait at the front door for Grace and Jack.

Whitford cleared his throat. "Thank you for gathering here today. Normally, we'd share the autopsy results with the next of kin, but in this case, Ms. Tremblay has agreed to share them directly with you as you've requested."

Lise stepped forward. "As Detective Whitford mentioned, I rarely make house calls, but in this instance, with all of you here, it made sense to answer any questions you may have."

Lillian leaned forward, a handkerchief twisted in her hands. "Should we wait for Grace and Jack?" Her voice was small, so unlike her usual confident self.

"Yes, of course," Lise replied. She took a seat, and Whitford pulled a chair up to the group, but just off to the side, looking stiff and uncomfortable. I brought him a cup of coffee with cream, no sugar, as I remembered he liked it. Freya appeared and nudged up against Whitford, but he ignored her. Not a cat lover, I guessed. Lise asked for a glass of water, appearing more relaxed than her colleague.

After a few minutes of awkward silence, I heard the front door open and Christie's voice greeting Grace and Jack. Soon they, too, sat with the group, warily staring at Detective Whitford, whose face was now deep red, a trickle of sweat across his broad brow. Lise, as always, remained perfectly composed, just as I remembered her before an important race. Totally focussed and unemotional.

"Now that everyone is here, I would like to share the pathology results with you," Lise said. The official cause of Richard Alcott's death was asphyxiation. He choked. Further investigation revealed he had inhaled strychnine, a poison that causes muscles to switch off, resulting in spasms and, in this case, asphyxiation and death." Lise paused and scanned the faces of the family members.

"Was the poison on the napkin?" I asked. Whitford glared my way, but Lise nodded.

"We analyzed the napkin, and it was likely the means for the strychnine to reach his lungs. It's not yet clear how that happened."

"That means ... someone did this to him?" Ian asked. He reached for Kate's hand, but she didn't move to receive it. Had they had an argument, or was her grief so strong that she didn't notice her husband reaching out to her?

Lillian dabbed her eyes with her handkerchief. "I just can't believe it. I thought he had taken his own life. Who would want to hurt Rick?"

Detective Whitford shifted in his seat, placing his empty coffee cup on the table. "We are investigating his death as suspicious. Thank you all for meeting with me, but I'd like to question everyone who was at the wedding and the rehearsal dinner, to start."

Grace nodded, visibly self-controlled. She'd matured so much since her brother's death. Now it was her turn to be strong for her husband. "I have a copy of the guest list, and so does Christie. I can email you my copy right away," she said, pulling out her phone.

Jack leaned his forearms on his legs; his head hung low. Grace reached over to touch his back. When he sat up again, his eyes were dry, but he was visibly shaken. "When did he die?"

"When Minna and Christie found him, he had already been there for between 24 and 36 hours," Lise replied.

"Around the time of the rehearsal dinner. He came to the rehearsal, but never made it. He was so close—" Jack released a sob and covered his eyes with his hand.

"We don't have all the details yet," Detective Whitford said.

Grace appeared confused. "But there was a note. Lillian told us he left her a note. I thought he died by—"

Whitford shook his head. "It's possible he poisoned himself. We haven't ruled out anything yet."

Grace slumped into her husband, who still couldn't face anyone. My heart reached out to them.

Lillian sat up straighter. "Thank you, Detective, and thank you, Ms. Tremblay. We appreciate you sharing this news with us personally."

Whitford and Lise said goodbye, and Christie and I followed them out to the driveway, leaving the family space to themselves.

"I don't get it. If Richard Alcott was coming to the rehearsal party, why didn't he change into his clothes before coming? He'd laid them out on the bed," I said. "I mean, he could have changed his mind and come how he was. Maybe he was running late?"

"How would you come by that information?" Whitford asked, crossing his arms and tilting his head in that familiar pose I'd become familiar with as a teenager.

"I ... I went to the cottages to look for him after the rehearsal dinner, but he wasn't there." I stuttered as I spoke, realizing I'd shared too much already.

"So far, we believe he checked into the cottage, drove to Hygge House, parked, and wandered to the lake. Took a seat in the Muskoka chair. At some point, he inhaled poison, either by his own hand or someone else's," Whitford said. His tone reminded me I should stay out of it.

"You don't need me to ask questions, do you?" I said, feeling rather sheepish.

"To be honest, Minna, I don't. Let us do our job. You may have solved one crime by fluke, but remember the deceased's family in there. They are all suffering. You do not need to lead them on a wild goose chase. Leave it to the professionals."

I bit my lower lip, deflated but understanding. "Okay, I hear you. I'm here to support the family and help you in any way you need," I said, confident that I meant it. "Just one more question. Did you find anything unusual in the cottage?"

"Nothing I can share with you." Whitford's shoulders lowered. "You have a business to run. Do your job and let me do mine."

Christie and I watched as Whitford pulled away in his police vehicle, and Lise Tremblay jumped into her SUV. "I can't handle another murder having happened at Hygge House," Christie said, leaning her shoulder against mine.

"Me neither. But we'll get through it. We always do," I said, less confident than I'd have liked.

Chapter 20

Lucy must have been busy this week at Winterberry and Willow Florists with all the orders. As with the wedding flowers, the funeral arrangements were stunning. I inhaled the scents and let the sounds of the organ wash over me as I took deep breaths to calm my nerves.

I squirmed in the hard pew, remembering the last funeral I'd attended was Owen Bradshaw's, and had a powerful urge to reach out to Grace. Considering the circumstances, she appeared composed, if a little pale and shaky. Beside her, Eloise looked stunning in a black dress and an oversized hat. Social media perfect.

As Jack stood up to read the eulogy, Grace held his hand for a few extra moments, and he wiped away the tears from his eyes, but as he started reading he commanded our attention, speaking with passion about the uncle he loved. Tears welled in my eyes as I remembered all of those we had lost over the years.

After Jack sat down, little Rosie sang "Amazing Grace" while Kate played the piano. I hadn't known the man, but funerals were always hard. I couldn't help but remember losing my father all those years ago. Beside me, Mom sat upright. I admired her stoicism during difficult moments. Must be her Finnish sisu that kept her going. I needed a little of that inner strength and resiliency just about now.

Just when I thought the service was over, Floyd and the members of Northern Spirit stood up and headed to the front of the church to play "Wish You Were Here." Norah's mournful voice had several people sobbing. I'm sure Richard Alcott would have appreciated his old bandmates' tribute. The song choice made me smile and remember my youth, but the tears kept flowing.

"You okay, Mom?" Sofia asked when the service ended, handing me a fresh tissue.

"Yeah, I'm good. The service was more emotional than I expected," I admitted. Christie sat on the other side of my mother and I could tell she, too, had struggled to stay composed during the service.

"Ready to go?" I asked. "Let's get back to the house before the guests arrive."

Christie smiled half-heartedly. "Good idea. And so I have time enough to fix my face."

A funeral following so shortly after a wedding wasn't in the plans, but we had to do what we could for the family. As I stood up, I scanned the church for James, but he was nowhere to be seen.

In the church parking lot, I looked up at the century-old structure with its tall spire and stained glassed windows. To the left, the old graveyard looked well cared for, with flowers and lanterns on many of the gravestones. I always loved to wander here, reading the names and dates of those long gone, but this time I shuddered. It was one thing to walk through years-old gravestones and another to be confronted by a newly prepared one.

I turned toward the car, only to see the band had gathered outside the church, and Eloise giving Norah a hug. The unlikely pair seemed to get on very well. Eloise really was a sweet girl.

Sofia, Mom, and I piled into my car, and we pulled out of the parking lot, headed toward Hygge House. James had agreed to transport the funeral flowers to the house in his truck. Perhaps he had left before us, and that's why I hadn't seen him in the church.

Taiga Hall was ready for the reception with the family and anyone who wanted to pay their respects, and Michael had finger sandwiches, vegetable and fruit platters, and desserts prepared. I recognized a few of his young servers, most of them in high school, from other events.

"Not exactly how I imagined starting summer," Christie said, straightening out a tablecloth.

"I know what you mean," I said. "Listen, everyone who is coming to the reception is someone who attended the wedding. I was thinking—"

"They're all suspects," Christie said. "Unless he really took his own life, in which case they're all just grieving friends and family."

"Just keep your eyes and ears open. If anyone lets something slip, let me know. If the murderer was at the wedding, he or she wouldn't skip the funeral. It would look too suspicious. Our pool of suspects is on that wedding list."

Christie agreed. "You got it, Sherlock. I'm on the case."

I grinned but then glanced around, conscious that guests would arrive at any moment. In fact, a moment later, Sofia opened the front door, and a large group drifted up the steps, entering Taiga Hall, and speaking in hushed tones. We greeted them solemnly, directing them to the food and inviting them to enjoy the garden as well.

As I was reorganizing the coffee station, Sofia sidled up, glancing around to make sure no one was hovering nearby. "What's up?" I asked, straightening the napkins.

"Do you remember the day Tyler and I went to play with the band?" She nodded toward the group chatting with Jack in the garden. It was nice that they paid respects to their former bandmate and supported the family.

"Yeah, you said Tyler enjoyed it," I replied.

Sofia nodded, but leaned in closer. "What I didn't tell you was that during the breaks all they could talk about was Rick. I should have told you then, but I didn't think much about it at the time."

"That makes sense. They were friends when they were young. They must be in shock." I thought about the first time a friend of mine had died and I'd attended her funeral. It was such a sad event. Life really was short and precious.

"But that's not all. I overheard Norah talking to Zander, and she sounded worried. Like, worried about Rick's death and what it meant for *him*."

My mother swooped towards us, refilling her teacup. "What's all this gossip?"

"Nothing, Mummu," Sofia said, glancing around again. "It's just that I heard some rumours about Zander, and I thought Mom would want to know."

"Who's Zander?" Mom asked, a little too loudly. Sofia and I both shushed her. Sofia pointed out the drummer, who had taken a seat with Grace in the garden.

"Oh, that lovely drummer. He's very good. I've heard him play at several community events. And he's handsome, too," she said, using that tone that suggested I should rush straight over and ask him out. My mother tilted her head and smiled as she does when she's pleased.

"He seemed overly concerned about Richard Alcott's death. He and Norah whispered about it when I went to hear them jam in Floyd's garage." Sofia rarely gossiped, so she must have thought it was important. Alarming, even.

"Well, that group goes back a lot of years. I remember the first time I saw them play at the Fall Fair. They were about fifteen or sixteen. Of course, Richard Alcott was the drummer back then."

I crossed my arms and inspected my mother's face. "You really know everything about this town, don't you?"

"Not everything. I don't know who murdered Richard Alcott," she said, shrugging.

"It may not have been a murder, Mom."

"Well, I don't think it was death by suicide. Do you believe that note? Even Lillian doubts it." Mom added some cream to her coffee and stirred it with a tiny spoon.

"She told you that?" I asked, exchanging a glance with Sofia.

"Not in so many words, but she's behaving a little suspiciously to me. Lillian knows more about her late-lover's death than she's saying. If that's the case, she'd want everyone to believe he took his own life, wouldn't she?"

"How do you know they were together?" I asked. I had told no one but Christie about my conversation with Lillian, not even my mom or Sofia.

"A woman sees things. At least anyone who is paying attention." My mother set her spoon down and took a sip of her coffee. "Off to chat with the bride and groom. I mean, the family of the deceased."

Sofia shook her head. "So, Lillian and Richard were in a relationship all this time? Does that make her—"

"A suspect? I'm thinking so." I squeezed Sofia's hand, and we headed outside to check on our guests, offering what condolences we could.

Chapter 21

Despite our best efforts, Christie and I learned nothing new at the funeral reception, but hosting it gave us an opportunity to grieve with the family and the community. Two days after the funeral, James and I sat in the breakfast nook, sipping coffee, but my mind was less on plans for renovating the space and more on Lillian.

"You seem preoccupied," James said, sitting back in his chair, his coffee mug propped on his knee.

"What? Oh, sorry. You were saying?" I said, dragging myself back to the present.

"I was suggesting flooring, but clearly there's something else going on with you. Want to talk about it?"

"Flooring, right." I glanced at the samples he'd brought. "This one," I said, pointing to a light-coloured sample that would be bright, but in a recycled material that would be easy to clean and do well in this three-season space.

"Exactly what I thought you'd choose," James said, chuckling as he made a note of the sample. "Its name is Scandi, so it tracks." He pulled out his measuring tape, and I stood up to hold the end while he measured and jotted the numbers in his notebook.

When we sat down again, he pulled out a brochure with window choices. I sighed.

"Okay, Minna. What's wrong? You usually love all these details. Sorting through paint chips and trim samples, but you just don't seem into it today."

"I'm sorry," I said. "You're absolutely right. I just need to focus." I sat up straighter and tried to clear my brain.

"Is it too difficult for you? Being in this space, I mean." James reached over to touch my arm, and tingles shot up from my toes.

He was right. It wasn't my favourite place. Not since I'd found Owen Bradshaw's dead body sprawled across the floor. The image of the young man shot across my vision, and I pushed it away. Would I ever be able to unsee it?

"Actually, I've been thinking about Lillian a lot these past few days." Instinctively, I glanced behind me, but the door to the kitchen was closed, and remembered Kate had taken Lillian and Rosie into town for a few hours. I didn't need to worry about being overheard.

"Do you want to fill me in?" James said. "You said Lillian read his last note. It must be hitting her hard."

"Yeah, I think so. She seemed very upset about the note, but it could be an act."

"You think *she* could have got him here and then killed him? On the day of her son's rehearsal party?" James looked incredulous.

I shrugged. "She's the one who convinced him to come here. And she's the only one who knew for sure he'd changed his mind several times. She claims not to know why he didn't want to come. If they were as close as she says they were, wouldn't he have explained it to her?"

James paused, his face pensive, telling me he was in deep-thought mode. It was hard not to smile at the indent between his brows when he was serious, or at that faraway look in his eyes. "Okay, let's think about the sequence of events." He opened his notebook to a fresh page. I liked the way this man thought.

"Rick wants to attend, but something is stopping him. He doesn't tell anyone, but he hints at it in a text to Jack. Lillian insists he comes, and he gives in to her demands. When he arrives on Friday, he meets someone in his cottage. Has a drink. A cigarette.

Doesn't change his clothes for the event. Flash forward, his car is in a visitor's space, his body is sitting in a Muskoka chair, and he's dead, asphyxiated by poison." He jotted down notes as he spoke.

I nodded. "And there is a note for Lillian on his bedside table suggesting he took his own life. Except I don't think he wrote it."

"If Lillian were responsible, would she have told him to meet her by the lake? Why wouldn't he arrive ready for the party?" James asked.

"If he died before getting to Hygge House, someone would have drove him here and brought him to the lakeside, propping him up in the chair." I can't picture Lillian having the ability to move a dead body. She's so petite, and Richard was not a small man.

"I have an idea," I said. James followed me outside to where Richard's car had been parked before the police removed it. "What do you notice?"

"Gravel? I don't know ..." James said, looking at the space. "What am I looking for?"

"Well, you'd expect to see footprints, right?"

"Sure, but we had rainfall the other day. That could have washed them away. I don't get it. Okay, Nancy Drew, explain your thinking," he said in that teasing tone he loves so much.

"Exhibit A." I pointed to a rake leaning against the outer wall. "The rake is usually in the garden shed, but someone has left it here." My mom, and Tyler when he works here, always put the tools away in the shed. She insists on it.

"Okay. Where are you going with this?"

I walked toward the Muskoka chair. "If I were dragging a body, I would want to cover my tracks. First, I'd rake the gravel to remove any footsteps near the car, and then after dragging the body, I'd rake the grass to remove evidence of dragging a body. Then, when you get closer to the lake, there's the smooth rock and the rocky shoreline where the chair sat. The suspect could have used the rake to remove evidence of footsteps down there, too."

"Hmm. I think you're onto something. But I still don't see how Lillian could have managed it by herself. They may have walked down there together, and she smothered him with the poison-soaked napkin. That way, no dragging involved."

"That would be much easier. I guess we need to get the time of death and whether the police recovered any footprints."

James raised an eyebrow. "Are you going to ask Whitford?"

"I'll ask Lise. She's more likely to share that information with me. But if Lillian is responsible, why would she want to kill the person she'd loved all those years?"

"And why did she keep it secret for all these years? She sounds like a suspect to me," James said as we wandered back up to the breakfast nook.

"She says she didn't want to upset her kids, but they haven't been kids for a long time. Hopefully, Lise will have more to tell me about his death. Can someone even poison *themselves* with a napkin?"

James picked up his coffee mug. "If anyone is going to find out, it will be you."

We returned to our plans for the renovation. James was right about one thing: a renovation here would make me more comfortable coming into the space. But it wouldn't get rid of the ghosts I feared were accumulating at Hygge House.

Chapter 22

I stopped by Grace's apartment the next morning, having promised her we could settle the bills, and with a plan to drive over to see Lise afterward. Fog rose from the lake as I took Lakeshore Drive towards the historic downtown and swung right a few blocks from Heritage Street to the apartment, now Grace and Jack's place.

At the top of the stairs, I paused outside the apartment door, hearing elevated voices. Just as I was about to knock, Jack opened the door, his eyes wide when he noticed me in the hallway. "Oh hey, Minna. I have to get to work. Nice to see you," he said, rushing past me. He seemed agitated and more than a little surprised to see me.

"Grace?" I asked through the open door. "Is this a good time?"

Grace appeared and nodded, but I could tell she'd been crying. She waved me in.

"Everything okay?" I asked, not wanting to pry, but the girl was clearly upset, and she must know I'd overheard them arguing.

Grace led me into her living room, somewhat less colourful than the last time I'd been there, and with a slightly more masculine feel. Jack had made his mark on the place.

"I'm fine. I guess you heard us bickering. The first one since the wedding, actually," she said. "I guess it was inevitable. Married couples argue too, don't they?"

I agreed. "How's Jack doing, after his uncle's passing?" I asked. I hated using euphemisms about death and dying, but somehow it just came out that way.

Grace slumped into an armchair and tucked her legs under her. "He's remarkably good. And that's exactly what we were squabbling about. It's like he didn't even care that his uncle died. He hasn't cried. He has shown no emotion since the funeral, as if it hadn't happened. When Owen died, I couldn't stop crying."

"He seemed shaken up at the service. Maybe he just processes his emotions differently," I suggested. I remembered sitting with Grace in this very place, eating Fika and Frosting cupcakes and talking about Owen. Owen's death shattered her, even though her brother had been a source of many disagreements between her and Jack.

"I guess, but just before the wedding, Jack was so angry. I've never seen him so upset with anyone, not even Owen. Jack loved his uncle, but his reaction to Rick's decision not to come to our wedding was, well, over the top. I told him to let it go. People have to make their own decisions, and we shouldn't hold it against him."

"Why didn't Rick want to come?" I asked, hoping to learn a little more. "His text said he didn't want to deal with the past. Do you know what he meant?"

She crossed her arms and stared out the window for a few moments. "Jack didn't tell me. I'm not sure he even knows."

I hesitated a moment, wondering how much I should ask, but Grace and I had already been through a lot, and I had her well-being at heart. "Grace, did Jack know that Lillian and his uncle were together?"

Her eyes widened. "No, I mean ... I don't think so." She took a moment to breathe. "Jack never told me about it, and Lillian didn't breathe a word until recently. Do you think Rick didn't want to attend because of her? I mean, I like my mother-in-law, but she can be a tough pill to swallow. Kinda controlling."

"Could Lillian be the past that he didn't want to revisit? Maybe it had nothing to do with Lakewood. If they had broken up, he might have resisted seeing her and only come after she insisted." Thoughts swirled around my head, images of Rick and Lillian, and a young Jack who must have noticed how much time they spent together. How could he not see what was going on in front of him? "And Jack never mentioned their relationship?"

"Not once. Rick was like a father to him, and naturally spent a lot of time with Lillian. If he suspected something, he's never said." She looked lost in thought.

From my purse, I pulled out the invoice. There was a small balance owing, but Christie and I had decided not to charge. Not after everything that had happened during their wedding weekend. I passed it to Grace.

"Oh, yes. How much do I owe you?" She glanced at the bottom of the invoice. "No, no. I need to pay you the balance. This is too much. You and Christie have already done so much for me and for Jack. For the wedding. And for the funeral reception."

I shook my head and smiled. "You and Jack don't need any further burdens. Take some time and go away for the weekend. Give yourselves a little honeymoon. Oh, and when you're ready, bring some of those beautiful handstitched vintage purses over. We're opening our little shop area for the summer."

Grace stood up and hugged me. "Thanks, Minna. Tell Christie I appreciate it. You two are really the sweetest."

We said our goodbyes at the door, and I made a silent plea to the marriage gods to look over these two. They'd been through too much already and deserved a happy life.

Chapter 23

The coroner's office was conveniently located a few blocks from the police station, close to Lakewood Hospital. I'd never been there before, and as I walked from my car to the main doors, a chill passed through me. How many dead bodies had been through this building? More than I cared to think about.

I entered the double doors to find a sterile hallway leading to the reception area.

"Is Lise Tremblay here?" I asked the young woman seated at her computer on the other side of the chest-height partition, suddenly aware I should have made an appointment.

"It's your lucky day," the receptionist said, peering at me over her 1950s style cat-eye glasses. She dialed a number and spoke in a quiet tone as I shifted from foot to foot. Perhaps this wasn't such a good idea after all.

A few moments later, Lise bounded through a set of doors towards me, a broad smile on her face. For someone who worked with dead people, she really was a ball of energy. I often saw her running on the trails or the boardwalk in the morning. Maybe I should take up jogging instead of walking with Hugo.

"Minna! So great to see you. I was just about to take a coffee break. Want some?" she said, motioning me to a room off the hallway. "Take a seat."

I set my purse on the floor and sat in the rounded orange plastic chair, more comfortable than it looked, and watched Lise put eco coffee pods in the machine.

"I'm guessing this isn't a social call," Lise said, beaming. I'd always liked her, even in high school when she was a junior and I was a senior. She was a track athlete then, and everyone recognized her, but she never boasted and was always kind to everyone.

"Not exactly. I appreciate the coffee, though. Actually, I had some questions about Richard Alcott's death. I'm not sure if you can help."

"You understand I can't tell you anything specific about the victim." Lise glanced toward the closed door. "But I could answer some general questions."

"Right. Okay, so hypothetically, if someone wanted to die by suicide, poisoning themselves, would they be able to put the poison on a napkin and hold it over their own mouth until they asphyxiated? Or would that not work at all?"

Lise sipped her coffee, a twinkle in her eye. "It's possible, but unlikely. The victim would probably panic and drop the napkin, at which time they might gasp for air or vomit, making the poison less effective."

"That makes sense. So someone else could hold the napkin over their mouth, causing them to choke?"

Lise nodded. "It's possible."

"Can I ask another question?" I leaned forward, cupping the coffee mug in my hands.

"Oui, of course." Something in our discussion made Lise sparkle. I'd once watched her do a presentation at the local library about forensics and couldn't help but get drawn in by her enthusiasm. She clearly loved this stuff.

"Richard didn't die of natural causes, and it's unlikely he could have done this to himself. Someone did this to him, right?" I was pushing the boundaries of what Lise could tell me, but I had to try.

"Your gut doesn't lead you astray, mon amie." Lise grinned.

"I'm curious. Did they find any footprints in the area?"

"Too many. You had many people there for the wedding and previous events. Some footprints were easily identifiable, but there were so many that it was impossible. But something curious caught my attention. The police said they found no footsteps from the car. Did the man just fly out of it? Who's to say?" Lise laughed and then stifled herself. "I should not laugh about death, or he may come for me next."

We chatted briefly, but Lise clearly had work to do, so I followed her out of the room and back into the reception area. I thanked her for her time and smiled at the cat-eyed receptionist. For a place that dealt with death all day long, they were certainly pleasant people, unlike the slightly less receptive Detective Whitford. Of course, Lise and I went back to high school, while Detective Whitford only remembered me as the kid who got in trouble with her best friend.

Chapter 24

That evening, James delivered drinks to our table and squeezed himself into the booth beside me. The sound of pool cues hitting balls in the adjoining room, accompanied by laughter and loud 80s music, reminded me of days spent playing pool here as young adults. Christie had tried to teach me, but I never quite got up to her level.

Christie took a sip of her drink, a fancy one with a pink umbrella, and glanced nervously at the door. "Do you think this is a bad idea? Floyd is practically old enough to be my father."

"He's older than you, but not that old. Besides, we're here to support you. It's not like this is a date or something." Despite my words, I was a little concerned. Floyd had taken a shine to Christie since our first meeting, and he was at least eight years older than us. But he seemed like a nice guy, someone you could rely on. At least I hoped so.

James raised his beer mug. "To a night out," he said, and we clinked glasses. I rarely went out in the evening, and then it was usually Boreal Beanery, after all that had happened over the last few weeks, it was nice to get away from all the talk of death and murder.

From the back room, a group raised their voices in greeting, causing us to look up. There was Floyd with his long beard and bright blue eyes, striding into the bar in his blue jeans, suede desert boots, and a tidy button-down shirt. Come to think of it, he'd make an excellent model for some trendy clothing brand for men.

Christie's face flushed as Floyd sat beside her, giving her a warm greeting. Could she really like this guy?

"Sorry, Floyd. We ordered drinks already. Can I get you something?" James asked.

Floyd nodded. "Same as you, pal. Thanks."

James went back to the bar to order. He was a good guy that way. Always ready to lend a hand. I turned my attention back to Floyd and Christie. For the first time in probably her whole life, it looked like Christie was tongue-tied.

"So, tell us about your band, Floyd. Everyone loved the music at the wedding reception," I said, trying to start the conversation.

"Yeah, it was so good," Christie chimed in like she was a teenage fangirl or something. "I haven't heard you all play in so long; I'd forgotten."

"Well, touring will do that. But it looks like we're back in town for good. Everyone wants to settle down for a while, so that means we'll play local gigs more often. I think you'll be seeing a lot more of me," he said, directing that last sentence to Christie, whose blush deepened.

"I was curious about something," I said, just as James delivered Floyd his beer and sat down. "I don't mean to talk about dark topics, but you mentioned Richard Alcott was once the drummer of your band."

Floyd raised his bottle. "To Rickie," he said, and we joined him. "Rickie Alcott was the best drummer this town has ever seen. Super bummed when he left. But things happen. Zander came along, and he's been a great addition."

"Yeah, he was amazing," Christie said. "But why did Richard leave back then?"

Floyd shrugged. "Yeah, he never really said. He had a thing for Norah, but she was dating Reggie."

"Is he in the band?" I asked. I thought I'd met all the band members at the wedding.

"Nah, not officially. Just fills in from time to time. When he and Norah broke up, he disappeared for years and worked out west—Alberta, I think. Now he lives out at Old Jackson's cabin on the outskirts of town."

I nodded. "Young lives were so complicated with everyone dating everyone."

"Yeah, we were all a little crazy back then. Thought we would make it big with our band, but as you can see, we're still just plugging away at it. It's been a good life, though. Wouldn't change a thing."

James took a sip of his beer and nodded over to a pool table that had just opened up. "Care for a game?"

"I'm in. You want to play on my team, Christie?" Floyd asked.

We wandered over to the table, and I watched James set it up. I hadn't played in so long; I wondered if I still remembered how.

"It surprised me to see Grace's young man here on the day of the rehearsal dinner," Floyd said, leaning over to line up his shot.

"Probably just settling his nerves before the big day," Christie said. "Do you remember when Jack was here?"

"Can't say exactly. I stopped in to pick up a cheque from George for playing a gig earlier in the week, and Jack and his best man—Harry, I think—were drinking and playing pool. I remember because I was on my way to Hygge House. Thought it was strange that one of the key players was here."

"Did he say anything?" I asked, taking my turn, and watching the balls careen across the table in every direction. I definitely needed more practice.

"Nah, I don't think he saw me. He was having a deep conversation with Harry, and I didn't want to interrupt them. Now that I think of it, he was looking pretty worried. Pre-wedding jitters, I guess."

Christie and Floyd beat James and me soundly. James just laughed and said, "We need more practice, Minna."

"You got that right," I replied. Christie and Floyd were chatting comfortably. Christie leaned up against the pool table, and Floyd was telling her some story or other. Perfect time to leave them on their own. James and I politely said goodnight and headed out.

"Is it weird that Jack and Harry came here before the rehearsal?" I asked.

"The timing is a little strange. What are you thinking?"

"Well, you might call me crazy, but Grace said Jack was really upset about his uncle not coming to the wedding. Do you think he went to confront him at the cottage before the wedding? Is that why he was looking so worried?" I couldn't quite put it together, but Jack might have had enough time to meet Richard, have a drink with him, then meet Harry at the pool hall.

"Are you saying Jack killed his own uncle?" James opened the passenger truck door, and I hopped in.

"I'm not saying that, but he was away from the house before the rehearsal. He could have done the deed and driven Richard's car back with Richard in it. At some point, he would have joined Harry. Perfect alibi."

James sighed. "You have quite an imagination, right? Why would a nephew murder his favourite uncle, right before his wedding?"

James was right. It was far-fetched, but who knew what could drive a person to murder? As James drove through the centre of town, I admired the fairy lights surrounding the oversized decorative flower pots and floral wreaths lining Heritage Street. The town really was pretty at night. One might even say romantic.

James turned right on Lakeshore Drive and headed toward Hygge House, its lights beckoning us through the tree-lined lane.

"Coming in for tea?" I asked as James swung around the circular drive, stopping in front of the front porch.

"Not tonight, but I'll be around tomorrow to get started on that breakfast nook. Are your guests still here?"

"With the funeral over, I think they'll be going home soon, but Lillian doesn't want to leave until she has more answers. Ian said he has to get back to work, and Kate wants to get Rosie home, too. We'll see."

"What about the influencer?" James asked.

"Eloise? She rescheduled her flight so that she could stay a few more days. She wants to support Grace, but all I saw her doing was taking videos and photos all over town. I guess Lakewood was good for her social media feed." I hated to admit it, but Eloise's Insta feed was beautiful, and she'd really presented Hygge House in the best light. The girl had talent.

We said goodnight. I turned to wave from the top of the steps and watched James's truck lights disappear down the lane. I plopped onto the porch swing and watched the fireflies dance in the distance. Solving this mystery would mean justice for Lillian, Richard's longtime love, and closure for Jack and Grace. The family could go on with their lives. I hoped.

Chapter 25

I pedalled down the boardwalk, glancing behind to check on Hugo, who was seated in his trailer. My phone pinged, but it was safely in my purse in Tuuli's basket. Probably Christie, wondering where I was. A few minutes later, I turned toward Heritage Street and then onto Lakeshore Drive, parking Tuuli beside the maple outside Vintage Pier. The scent of lilacs wafted in my direction.

Christie opened the door and frowned. "Took you long enough. I could have picked you up from Hygge House," she said. Christie didn't quite understand my love of nature. She was more of an indoor girl overall.

"What? And miss this amazing weather? We spent all year waiting for summer, and now it's here and you want to drive your car." I couldn't help but laugh at her *who me?* expression. Of course, we both knew the truth. At least I could convince her to go for forest walks with me occasionally.

Priya greeted me warmly as we entered the store, leaving Hugo to enjoy a shady spot under the tree. "What are you two looking for today?" She leaned against the counter Dev had constructed out of a vintage bar. "Anything special for Hygge House?"

"The Horticultural Society is having its Midsummer Garden Party tomorrow, and my mom has decided she needs some decorative garden accessories. We thought we'd start here," I said. "A chance to see you and catch up."

Priya grinned, and we chatted as we headed to the back of the store.

Christie was wandering around aimlessly, touching items briefly and frowning. "What are we looking for exactly? Did Elsi give any directions? Maybe a list?"

"Good question. Mom said to find some 'cute summer things to create interest around the garden beds,'" I said, checking my phone messages for the details.

"You're in luck. Follow me," Priya said. "I have a few garden gnomes and water features." She led us toward the back room, where they had a display of summer items under a large garden umbrella strung with lights.

"Now that's what I'm talking about," Christie said, her countenance brightening. "Feels so summery here. What do you think we should focus on?"

I took a few moments to scan all the items. "Why don't we just get a bunch of stuff, and Mom can decide what she wants to use?"

"That's a good idea. Just bring back anything you don't need," Priya suggested. I loved how easy she made it to shop at Vintage Pier.

I selected a set of garden chimes, a trio of fairies in various poses, some little fairy doors to put at the base of trees, and an ornate sundial. Christie picked up a laughing Buddha, a birdbath, and bedazzled fairy garden stakes.

"Any news about Richard Alcott?" Priya asked as she rang up our items at the cash. "Dev heard a rumour that he didn't die of natural causes, like we all assumed." Priya spoke in hushed tones. There were a few young women checking out the vintage clothes and an older couple wandering near the furniture in the back. I appreciated her discretion.

I glanced at Christie, and she shrugged. The whole town probably heard the details, and Priya was Grace's friend. "The coroner says he died of poisoning, but the question is whether he did it to himself or someone did it to him."

Priya's eyebrows raised. "Another murder at Hygge House?" She looked as alarmed as I'd been.

"Unfortunately, yes. I know what you're thinking. It's not good publicity for our fledgling business," I said. "But there is nothing we can do about it. We just have to keep going."

"And Minna is an amazing sleuth. She'll have it solved in no time," Christie said, nudging me playfully.

I gently shoved her away. "First, I'm an interior designer, not a sleuth. And I am not actively involved in this case. The police have it well under control." Did the lady protest too much? Perhaps.

Priya's eyes sparkled. She leaned her elbows on the counter, and propped her head in her hands. "So you have no leads for this one, Minna? As I recall, you had lots of theories about Owen Bradshaw's death."

"Well ... I have been wondering about a few things. Like, where was Jack before the rehearsal dinner? Floyd saw him with Harry at the pool hall, but he wasn't there the whole time, apparently." I scratched my head.

Christie nodded enthusiastically. "I forgot to tell you. During my date with Floyd—"

"You had a date with Floyd Beck from Northern Spirit?" Priya interjected. "Huh." She appeared puzzled, but not dismayed.

"Yes, I did. And while we were chatting, Floyd told me more about the early days of the band, kind of reminiscing about the good old days. I think he was feeling sentimental, what with Richard gone. He figured Rickie—as he called him—was lovesick for Norah, but Norah was dating someone else. He's not sure what happened, but they had an argument and things were never the same."

"And that's when Rickie—I mean, Richard—left the band?" Priya asked. "That's so romantic. Like some old 1980s movie where the boy loves the girl who loves someone else. Like Ducky in *Pretty in Pink.* Did Norah and Rickie ever get together?" Priya had a dreamy look in her eyes. A romantic, if ever there was one.

"Not that I'm aware of. Sounds like when Richard left, he left for good. And Floyd had a hard time with it. He did everything he could to make Zander feel comfortable, but in his eyes, Zander was no Richard Alcott. But they're all good now, of course."

"Huh," I said. "Floyd sounds like a real softy."

Christie smiled. "Yeah, he's a teddy bear. Anyway, it probably has nothing to do with anything, except that Floyd really loved the guy and is having a hard time with his death."

"Keep me posted," Priya said. "I just can't believe Grace is dealing with another death so soon after her brother's. And let me know if there is anything I can do to help."

"You got it," I replied, giving Priya an appreciative smile. Armed with our garden accessories, Christie and I said goodbye.

"Oh, and I'll be at the garden party tomorrow if you need anything. I'm bringing Grace. She needs a day out." Priya waved from the door. The townsfolk of Lakewood really looked out for one another. My heart was full of gratitude.

We piled the items into the trunk of Christie's car, parked across the road, the aroma of fried fish and vinegar from the Fish 'n' Chips shop nearby making my mouth water.

"I'm starving. How about lunch?" I suggested.

Christie agreed, and we strolled over to the shack, brightly painted yellow with blue trim. I couldn't remember a time when it hadn't drawn locals and tourists alike. Thankfully, the lineup was short.

We found a picnic table under a tree, and we sat facing the lake. Hugo sat prettily, waiting for me to share a fry with him, and I willingly obliged. "Summer in Lakewood has to include fish and chips."

"Right?" Christie agreed through a mouthful. "This place is usually so packed; it's nice to have it to ourselves today."

"You didn't say how your date went," I said, dipping a fry into ketchup.

"I just told you and Priya what we talked about." Christie stuck her fork into a battered piece of fresh fish.

"Yeah, but you didn't talk about how the date part went. Did you have a good time? Do you like him?"

"What? Am I fifteen years old again?" Christie shook her head, then broke into a smile. "Actually, I had a lovely time. We got along great. The guy could be my father—well, my older brother anyway—but I had fun."

"Okay," I said, turning my attention bag to Hugo, who was relentless with delicious-smelling human food. "You seemed very relaxed with him when James and I left. Are you going to see him again?"

Christie gazed over the sparkling water, and I watched her expression shift slightly. "Maybe."

"So you're finally giving up your dating app?"

"Now, just hold on a minute. I didn't say we were that serious," Christie said, hugging her phone to her chest.

It might be some time before Christie decided about Floyd, and that was okay with me. There was no reason to rush into anything. I needed to wait until she wanted to share her feelings with me instead of pressuring her. We'd been friends for long enough for me to understand when to give her space.

Chapter 26

T he next day, the Horticultural Society arrived in droves, taking over the garden and the lakefront patio. My mother directed traffic, telling folks where to set up their tables and tents, and ensuring everything was aesthetically pleasing for the attendees as they strolled through the yard and into the garden. To my surprise, Lillian was buzzing around, helping the vendors set up their booths. Two peas in a pod, as they say.

The event was a fundraiser for the society, which handled the town's gardens and Heritage Street's planters throughout the year, so Christie and I had given them the space as our contribution. Luckily, that meant we didn't have too much to do in terms of setup. The members brought everything they needed, and Mom's efficient organizational skills came to great use.

"Thank goodness for Elsi," Christie said. We stood in the breakfast nook overlooking the garden. James had pulled out the flooring and brought the walls down to the studs, but he still had a lot of work to do before he brought it back to life. Already, I was feeling more comfortable in the space.

"Right? Where does she get the energy?" I hoped I'd have as much vigour at her age. "Oh, there's Sofia and Tyler. Let's give them a hand."

We strode across the lawn where the two were setting up a lemonade stand, complete with cupcakes from Frosting and Fika.

"Are Amanda or Terri coming?" I asked. I'd thought the couple would be here selling their goods.

Sofia shook her head. "We're taking care of their booth today. Amanda's taking care of the bakery, and Terri's visiting her sister in Birchtown. They're donating all the proceeds to the society. Besides, it will be fun for us."

"Yeah, plus check out this baking." Tyler opened a box of gluten-free cupcakes and used a hand to waft the vanilla scent my way.

"Yum. I'll be back for one of those later. Save me one with chocolate and peanut butter, please. Anything we can help you with?" I asked.

"We have a few more boxes of goodies in the truck," Sofia said. "Can you carry some over?"

"No worries. I've got them," Tyler said. He grinned at me and strode toward the Lakewood Catering truck he'd borrowed from Michael. I appreciated Tyler's can-do attitude. Christie and I helped Sofia display the items and make sure the iced tea and lemonade were ready for the guests. Already the day was heating, and it promised to be a hot one.

"Sofia, I was wondering about something you said. When you went to watch Tyler play with Northern Spirit, you said Norah and Zander were arguing. Do you remember anything about their conversation?" Just as I asked, Mom sauntered towards us, dressed in a lovely cream linen skirt and top, with strappy sandals, and a large-brimmed hat encircled with flowers over her silver bob. Suddenly, I felt like I should change into something more garden party and less dig-in-the-dirt.

"What's all this about Norah and Zander?" she asked.

"It's just that I learned Richard Alcott was in love with Norah when they were young, but she was dating someone else. Broke his heart," I said. "And Norah and Zander ended up dating after that relationship ended."

My mom straightened out the tablecloth and adjusted a garden fairy standing with its wings perked up and its wand stretched out over a flower. If only I could wave a wand and have some magic happen, this investigation would be behind us all.

"That was a very long time ago, and you remember I had a young person of my own to raise. I wasn't paying much attention to the teenagers in town. Although that band got into some trouble, as I recall." Mom shook her head and raised a hand to her temple. "I'm trying to remember ... it will come back to me ..."

Mom always had an excellent memory of the townspeople and the town's history, but she was getting older, so it was natural the memories might take a little longer to download.

"No worries. If you think of anything—"

"Yes, yes. I'll tell you right away," she said. She glanced at her vintage silver watch. "The master gardener will be here within the hour, and I want everything to be just right before he arrives to judge the entries. Of course, I'm not sure the competition can stand up to what I have this year." She gave us a mischievous smile before wandering toward Sally's table of begonias.

Sofia opened the last box from Fika and Frosting and organized the sweet treats, including Nanaimo bars, raisin cookies, and blueberry tarts, on the table, while Tyler stacked the cups, ready for the lemonade and blueberry iced tea.

"Do you really think Zander or Norah had anything to do with Richard's death? I mean, it must have been forty years ago that Richard was in the band," Sofia asked.

"Yeah, it's probably nothing, but they keep coming up, so I can't help but think one of them knows something about what happened to Richard."

Christie raised an eyebrow and pointed towards the house with her chin. "Look who's here. You can ask them yourself."

To my surprise, Norah had arrived, dressed in a black sundress and straw hat, along with black Doc Martens. Zander followed behind. I waved and handed my gardening gloves to Christie. "Be right back," I said, striding towards her.

At the other end of the garden, Eloise was taking a selfie with Priya and Grace in front of the bridal arch. Clearly, Henri's arch was drawing people over. A small line had formed, waiting their turns to take the perfect picture.

"Norah, I didn't expect to see you today," I said.

"Actually, Elsi invited us when we played at the wedding, and I promised to drop by. Besides, I need some planters for my front porch." She glanced around, and noticing Grace with her friends, turned away, a slight frown on her face.

"Sounds like Mom. She's big on supporting town events and will grill you if you don't turn up. Let me show you where the hanging baskets are located." I led her towards the section of the lawn where the horticulturists displayed the baskets. "I haven't seen you since the wedding. So sorry about Richard. I heard you two were close." I needed to tread carefully here. Norah might not like my prying into the past.

"I wouldn't say we were close, to be honest. He was a nice guy, but I was sometimes a little uncomfortable around him. He kind of mooned over me when we were kids. Who can blame him? I was pretty hot as a teenager." Norah laughed aloud, clearly not taking herself seriously, and I laughed along. "But seriously, I'm sorry he's gone." Norah looked appropriately sad about it, but did she really miss him?

"My mistake. I got the impression that he left the band because the two of you had a fight."

Norah's cheeks reddened, and she turned away. "I don't remember ever arguing with him. He left. We moved on without him. I broke up with the other guy anyway and then started dating Zander." She pointed to him a few feet away, pretending to look at the pansies, but I suspected he was really listening to our conversation. "Zander and I have been on and off again over the years. But we always stayed friends."

"It's great when high school friends stay in touch. Did you keep in contact with Richard once he moved away?"

"No, we lost touch after he left. You know, the occasional phone call, but he never visited."

I nodded. "Yeah, that happens a lot when people part ways. Life keeps going, and it's hard to maintain close friendships. But your band has done great." Thankfully, Christie and I had stayed close over the years.

"The core band has been together for decades, but some folks come and go. And some come back to play a few gigs now and again, like Reggie and a few others. Speaking of gigs, we have one at a cottage this weekend. Why don't you come along?" Norah grabbed my arm. "It will be so fun."

"Really? Won't the owner mind?" I asked.

"Not at all. We're the entertainment for the evening, and everyone's invited. The more the merrier," Norah said. "I'll text you the address. Bring whoever you want." She flashed a smile like she'd done on stage and picked up two baskets. "Oh, look. Just what I needed. Nice chatting with you, Minna," she said, handing the baskets to Zander before paying Sally.

Just then, Eloise sauntered over with her phone held up. "Norah! Would you mind taking a selfie with me?" Norah murmured something I couldn't hear and strode away before anyone could say another word. Eloise looked hurt.

"I guess she doesn't like social media," I said, agreeing to a selfie by the lilac bush.

Eloise frowned. "She's a boomer. They don't always get social media. She should take my new online course. It's designed for that age group. Hey, Minna, why don't you take it, too?"

"Um, I'm Gen X, but thank you," I said, trying to squash my amusement. Besides, I had Sofia to help with social media when I needed it. And honestly, I considered myself pretty tech savvy. Kinda.

"I've made glowing comments about the property, and it wouldn't surprise me if you get reservations from overseas. My flight is later tonight, so I just wanted to thank you and Christie for your hospitality. I really appreciate everything you're doing for Grace and Jack." Eloise gave me a hug.

As uncomfortable as I was with hugging, I returned it. "You are welcome back anytime. It was a pleasure."

"Don't you worry. I'll be back." Eloise's smile beamed, and she turned back towards Priya and Grace, leaving me alone again. To tell the truth, I might not be a boomer, but I didn't really get social media either. I just knew it was necessary for our business, and sometimes I spent too much time scrolling through the feed.

I wandered around the yard, checking out the tables and tents, and admiring my mother's garden, where she was giving a tour. The master gardener was taking notes on his clipboard—Christie would love that—and chatting with the participants. It wasn't clear how he would select the winners. It was beyond me. But so were all the complicated relationships Norah had with her bandmates. And just because she was a serial monogamist didn't mean she had anything to do with Richard Alcott leaving the band. But could she be the reason he didn't want to come back? Had he still been in love with her? Is that what he'd argued about with Lillian?

In the distance, I spied James chatting with his father, Henri. I took a cue from Eloise and ambled over to him, hoping he'd agree to come to the house party with me. It would give us a chance to hang out and even chat with the band a little more. I suspected they knew more about Richard's death than they were saying.

Chapter 27

James parked at the end of a long string of cars curving along the narrow dirt road leading through dense foliage toward the cottage. When I opened the door, it was clear we were in the right place. Music drifted towards us, along with laughter from the guests who had already arrived. Twinkle lights adorned the trees toward the cottage, leading the way and creating a warm ambience.

"Wow, would you just look at that place?" James said, emitting a low whistle. "I was expecting a camp or a small cottage, but this is a mansion."

We paused a few feet away from the multi-tiered deck. On one level, the band had set up facing the lake. A group was already using the rest of the space as a dance floor. A level down, folks sat at tables, enjoying a wide variety of beverages. Yet another tier, and more guests were hanging out on the deck close to the lake. A few steps down brought them to the dock and a covered boathouse housing an expensive-looking speedboat and three Sea-Doos, plus other toys like stand-up paddleboards and fishing gear.

"This really is something. Who owns it?" I asked.

James shrugged. "Beats me. I thought I knew everyone in town. Could be a holiday home. Some Toronto tycoon."

Someone behind us cleared his throat, and we turned to see a neatly dressed man in shorts and a short-sleeved button-down shirt. "The tycoon would be me, I guess," he said, holding out his hand. "Sorry, I didn't mean to overhear you."

Even though the lights were dim, I could see James blush. "Sorry, man. I didn't know—the place is beautiful. Great craftsmanship."

"Hey, no problem. I'm Evan Lahti. Nice to meet you both," he said. We introduced ourselves. "Are you interested in architecture? I can give you the tour."

James immediately took him up on it, but I declined. "I'm going to see if Christie's here. I'll catch up with you later," I said to James.

The band had just finished its set, and I wanted to see who was around to chat. I noticed Tyler was playing, but Sofia had mentioned nothing about coming to the party. Beside Tyler, a man with a big beard and deep lines on his face was playing the guitar. Jed wasn't playing, so this must be his replacement, Reggie.

I took the closest steps to the second tier, weaving between the tables and saying hello to the townsfolk I recognized. In one corner, I noticed Priya sitting with Amanda and Terri. She waved me over, but I shouted I'd be back soon.

On the top tier, the dancers were taking a break, some ordering drinks at the makeshift bar, while the band put down their instruments.

"Minna, you came. So happy to see you," Norah said, looking genuinely pleased.

"I wouldn't have missed it. I rarely get a night out these days."

Floyd noticed me and stepped towards us. "Did you bring Christie?" Floyd asked with a familiar glimmer in his eyes.

"As a matter of fact, I was just looking for her myself. She should be here any minute. And Evan Lahti is giving James the tour as we speak."

"Good man, that Evan," Floyd said. "Big-city guy with a small-town heart. He inherited this property from his grandfather, Olavi Lahti. Evan used to come up here as a kid and spend the summers. Now he's built his dream palace, even though he spends most of his time in the city. Reckon he'll retire here someday."

"If he ever retires," Norah said. "That man is driven by capitalism, but there's hope for him still. We keep telling him to slow down and enjoy life a little more. He says he'll slow down when he dies."

"Some people just have a lot of energy, I guess," I said.

"Have you met Reggie yet?" Floyd asked, pointing toward the guitarist.

When he heard his name, Reggie turned around like a big bear lumbering in our direction. He nodded at me politely, but didn't offer any greetings.

Floyd grinned. "Reggie joins us now and again, but he hasn't been a regular member of the band since ... when, Norah?"

"Oh, late 80s, I guess," she said. "I'm going to get some water. Need anything?" She didn't seem to be interested in a conversation with or about Reggie. That made sense since they were exes after all.

"I'm going to see if Christie's around," Floyd said. "See you later."

That left me milling around the stage, Tyler having drifted off and Zander nowhere in sight. "Floyd says you play with the band sometimes," I said, feeling foolish to say something so obvious.

Reggie sat on a round bench and took a sip from his bottle. "Yeah, still love to play, but don't like crowds much." He glanced around at the party-goers and clearly looked uncomfortable. "Heard you bought the old historic house on Long Lake."

"Sure did. My business partner, Christie, and I are doing a lot of renovations. Well, James Evergreen is really the one doing the work, but I'm an interior designer, so that's my contribution." I felt like I was rambling. How was I going to turn this around to ask about Richard? I paused and stared out at the lake for a minute. "I guess you heard about the death at Hygge House."

"Rickie Alcott? Sure did," Reggie said, shaking his head. "Damn shame. We hung around a lot as kids. Back in the days when Norah was my girl." I followed his gaze across the makeshift dance floor, where Norah and Zander were chatting with a small group. Was that regret I noticed?

"What happened back then? Why did Richard leave the band?" I asked, treading carefully.

"Why does anyone do anything? He moved out of town shortly after quitting. Maybe that was always the plan for him. He'd outgrown our childish nonsense. No idea," Reggie said. "Zander had to work hard to catch up with Rickie. He was a genuine talent. Like a young Phil Collins or Neal Peart."

"Strange that Richard didn't pursue music after he moved away," I said. "I wonder why."

"His parents didn't think music was an actual career, and his brother Pat was studying to be a doctor or a lawyer or something. Rickie looked up to him. Probably felt the pressure all around. What a waste."

It occurred to me that Reggie understood something about Richard Alcott that the others couldn't express. Their youthful friendship went deeper than some of his other relationships, even though he seemed well-liked.

Just as I was about to ask about Richard and Lillian's relationship, Floyd arrived and, as if on cue, the other members of the band congregated on the stage and started a rendition of "Summer of 69" by Bryan Adams. It didn't take long before the dance floor filled and people were singing along.

By the end of the song, James had found me sitting with Priya and Christie while Terri and Amanda danced. He grabbed a chair and pulled it close. "This house is amazing. Evan has really done a great job of incorporating local craftsmanship and modern elements. Plus, he kept his grandfather's original building for guests. It's like a time capsule. Brilliant."

"Yeah, it's really beautiful inside," Christie said.

"Wait, you know Evan Lahti?" I asked.

Christie shrugged. "We had a few dates, but it didn't go anywhere."

"Huh." I took a drink and stared at my friend, still able to surprise me. I guess being away meant I didn't know everything Christie got up to. While the idea of touring Evan's mansion-like cottage was appealing to the designer side of me, I couldn't keep my eyes off the band. These deep connections had been going for decades, and somehow Richard Alcott was still a vital part of them, despite his years of absence.

A few hours later, the crowd was thinning, and only the young people were still dancing like they had all night. When had I become so old that I longed for my pillow?

"I'm ready to go when you are," I said to James, who was stifling a yawn. At least he felt his age as much as I did.

"Home already?" Priya asked. "The night is young."

"I'm afraid my bed is calling me," I said. "But Christie's staying, right?"

Christie agreed. "A little longer. Floyd said he'd drive me home."

I said goodnight and waved to Terri and Amanda in the distance. The band was on a break, and I wondered how they could stay up so late. I guess by sleeping until noon.

As we rounded the corner of the cottage, heading toward James' truck, voices from behind the house stopped me in my tracks.

"I don't want to see him again," a woman's voice said, sounding distressed.

"I get it, but let's get you home before things get out of control," a male voice replied.

"That sounds like Norah." I grabbed James's arm. "We should check on her."

Before we could intervene in the argument, Zander appeared, holding Norah up.

"Is she okay?" I asked, rushing towards her.

Zander kept his arm around her waist, with her arm slung over his shoulder. "She's a little incoherent. I think she has food poisoning."

"Do you need help?" James asked, stepping forward.

Zander shook his head. "I already told Floyd I'd bring her home. Make sure she's okay. She'll be alright."

We watched them stagger towards Zander's car, and he helped her in. I'd never seen her like this before, but then I didn't know her that well. In fact, at the wedding she drank only water the whole night.

James held the truck door open for me. "I don't miss those days."

"What? The fall-over-drunk days? Party-all night? The after-the-night-before feeling?"

"All the above," James said. "Not that I was much of a partier, but I have no desire to revisit any of my youthful indiscretions."

I laughed. "I wish I'd known you then. Norah's not very youthful anymore. She's older than I am."

"That will make recovery tomorrow even harder, I bet." James turned on his truck and turned around to head home. "If I'd known you then, I don't think either of our lives would have been the same." He leaned over and turned on the radio, his driver-side window open, letting in the night air.

I wanted to respond, but let the warm feeling of possibilities embrace me. Ah, to be young again. But no, I wouldn't go back for anything.

Chapter 28

I poured myself a second cup of coffee and leaned against the kitchen island. I would need it to get through the day after staying up so late the night before, but I promised I'd help James with the windows for the breakfast nook. By the time I'd added my cream, he was knocking at the back door.

"Coffee?" I asked. Hugo Dogberg, my little shadow, followed me to the coffeemaker.

"Always," he answered. "I'm feeling a little groggy this morning, I must admit." Despite his statement, he looked pretty refreshed, whereas I felt like the proverbial truck had run me over. Maybe twice.

I found a large mug and poured him a cup of black coffee, just the way he liked it. "I wonder how Norah's feeling this morning. Should I call her?"

"I guess that would be nice of you, but she probably just wants to sleep in. You know what these musicians are like. They keep odd hours."

"Yeah, you're probably right. And it's not like we're close or anything. I was just worried about her." We headed into the breakfast nook, where James had left his tools.

James had arranged the new windows at the far end, still in their wrappings, and he'd already removed the old ones the day before, covering the openings with clear plastic in case we had rain overnight. He started by removing the plastic, letting in the fresh morning air. I breathed in deeply.

He positioned the first window into the slot left by the old; my job was to hold it in place. It didn't take long before he had it secured and moved to the next one. He'd do the finishing work later, he'd said.

On the third window, I heard a car pull up to the side of the house where we parked, the same place we'd found Richard Alcott's car. The police had found no fingerprints in the car to suggest someone else had been driving it. That shot down that idea.

Footsteps rounded the corner. It was Christie, looking drained of colour.

"You okay?" I asked. "Did you stay out too late?" Could she be sick? I hoped she hadn't gotten food poisoning or caught what I'd had earlier. Summer flus were the worst.

Christie slumped into a chair and buried her hands in her face. It was unlike her to be speechless.

"Okay, now you're scaring me. Did something happen? Are you okay?" I knelt beside her chair and touched her knee.

Christie slowly sat up, her eyes welling with tears. "Norah Kincaid is dead."

I gasped, and James staggered, reaching out to grab my arm. "What happened?"

"I'm not sure. Floyd called me this morning. The ambulance came, but they couldn't revive her. The police arrived soon after to investigate."

"But we saw her last night," I said, remembering her inability to walk, her drunken state. Or a drugged state. "Didn't you say Norah stopped drinking years ago?"

Christie nodded. "Floyd mentioned she'd been clean for three decades. She ate well, exercised. Really, she was in remarkable shape." For her age, I added in my head.

"When James and I were leaving, she was in a terrible state. She looked intoxicated." I glanced at James, who nodded to confirm.

"I doubt that. She was a real health nut. Why would she go back now?" Christie said, her eyebrows furrowing. "Do you think—"

"Someone drugged her? Or poisoned her?" Who would want to kill Norah? If Norah knew something about Richard Alcott's death, they may have needed to get rid of her, too.

"Are you thinking what I'm thinking?" Christie asked, gazing at me with those expectant eyes.

"Yeah, I am. James, can you handle this on your own?"

James glanced at the last few windows. "Sure thing. I'll text Tyler and see if he can help me out with the remaining few." He didn't look upset that I was abandoning him to finish the job alone.

"They look so good," Christie said, admiring our work. "I love this space so much more already." Her positive comments did not mask how devastated she sounded.

We left Hugo, who was more than happy to observe James working, and headed towards her car. Christie popped into the driver's seat. "Okay. What's the plan?"

I paused for a moment as I buckled in. "Let's head to Norah's house first. We might find out what happened to her."

"You got it, Sherlock," Christie said, backing up and turning into the circular driveway.

Norah lived in a small house a few kilometres from the town centre in a quiet residential neighbourhood. Her house must have been over a hundred years old, but well maintained. The flower baskets she'd bought at the horticultural event were hanging from hooks on either side of the porch steps and looked a little wilted. The empty porch swing hung on the left, and a set of chairs and a small bistro table on the right appeared lonely.

What made the place most unsettling were the police cars parked in the driveway and officers consulting one another on the lawn. I'd seen this scene too often lately. Did they all need to be here? Apart from Norah's death, it was probably a quiet day for crime in Lakewood, and they had nowhere else to be.

Christie parked on the road, and we headed toward the house. I'd expected some police tape to restrict us, or someone to stop us, but no one blinked an eye as we approached.

Detective Whitford appeared at the front door and, seeing us, frowned. He strode our way. "Minna. Christie," he said, nodding politely.

"Detective Whitford, we just wanted to—" I started.

"Interfere? I'm surprised it took you so long to get here. I expected you earlier."

I couldn't tell whether he was teasing us or reprimanding us. "We don't want to get in the way. It's just Norah died so soon after Richard Alcott's murder. That can't be a coincidence."

Whitford shrugged and scratched the stubble on his beard. "Why would you think the two deaths are connected?"

Christie snorted. "Why would you think they aren't? Did you know Richard was in love with Norah back in the day?"

"I don't see how that's relevant. It's a small town." Whitford seemed unmoved.

"And they used to play in a band together?" I said.

"Northern Spirit has been around for decades. People come and go from bands all the time. I'm not at all surprised that they played together. You need something more substantial, ladies."

"Was it foul play?" I asked, crossing my arms and looking him square in the eye.

Whitford shuffled his feet and looked uncomfortable. "I can't reveal any details yet, but ... her death warrants an investigation."

"I knew it," Christie said, almost gleefully. "I mean, it's a terrible loss for the community."

"Uh-huh. If you'll excuse me, I have some work to do," Whitford said.

"Right. Thank you, detective," I said, grabbing Christie's arm and leading her back to the car. "So, we have two things confirmed. One, Norah's death was not natural and not an accident.

It was foul play. Two, we have one less suspect for the death of Richard Alcott."

Christie frowned and hugged her body with her arms. "And that also means the murderer is still out there and might target anyone who suspects what happened. That makes us all potential targets."

I hadn't thought of it that way. I shivered despite the day's warm breeze, and we jumped back in the car.

Chapter 29

As Christie navigated Lakeshore Drive back toward Hygge House, I gazed at the lake, the sun bouncing off the ripples and the water shimmering. My idea that Norah had been involved in Richard's death had come to nothing. The circumstances stumped me.

Christie opened her driver-side window and let in the warm breeze. "I'm thinking whoever killed Norah must also have got to Richard Alcott, too."

"My thoughts exactly. But what did Norah have to do with it? She dated Richard all those years ago, but I don't see that as a reason for her involvement. Do you think she knew something about his death?"

Christie shrugged, her hands gripping the wheel as we pulled into the long driveway. A beat-up old van with stickers from different provinces and states covered the back door.

"Whose car is that?" I asked.

"Floyd's. They use it on tour to lug around their equipment. Not much to look at, but that van has seen a lot of places over the years."

Christie parked in her usual spot at the side of the house, and from there we could see Elsi and Sofia sitting with Floyd on the covered patio. He could be here to see Christie, but his presence made my stomach squeeze.

"Floyd, what are you doing here?" Christie asked. While I was contemplating how to greet him, she, as usual, just came out with it. Introverts need extroverted friends.

Floyd stood up to greet us and sat down again as we pulled chairs up to the table.

"Sofia and I have been having a most pleasant time with Floyd," Mom said. "He's had a rough time of it. I'll get some coffee cups for the two of you two." From the stack of mail beside her coffee cup, she pulled out an envelope addressed to me.

"Who is it from?" Sofia asked, eyeing the envelope. The address was in perfect calligraphy. "Looks like a wedding invitation."

"No idea. I don't see a return address," I said, turning it over in my hands before placing it beside my coffee cup for later. "Is James still here?" I asked as Christie and Floyd exchanged pleasantries.

Sofia shook her head. "He and Tyler went to Henri's to pick up some things for the windows. They should be back soon."

After Mom returned and poured everyone more coffee, we sat back in silence for a few moments. Wind rustled through the trees, sunlight trickled onto the verandah, and the scent of lilacs wafted our way.

"I'm sorry for your loss, Floyd," I said. "Norah's been an important part of your life for decades."

Floyd nodded solemnly. "She was a good person." He shook his head and stared at his hands, calloused from years of playing. "Who would do this to her?"

Christie reached out and covered his hands with hers. "We're going to figure this out. I promise."

There was that word again. How could we promise anything to this man, who was grieving for his long-time friend and bandmate? But deep in my heart, I felt we had to try.

"Losing loved ones is so difficult," my mother said, placing a riisipiirakka on a plate. She sliced a piece of Jalsburg cheese and placed it on top, and handed the plate to Floyd. "Eat, eat."

Floyd accepted her offerings and took a bite. "Delicious, Elsi." He took a sip of coffee, his downward cast eyes revealing his deep distress.

Mom smiled sympathetically and looked pleased with herself, running her hand through her freshly cut hair. Whenever there was a crisis, she remained calm—and offered food. No one would go hungry in an emergency if my mother was around.

James's truck pulled up beside Christie's car. He and Tyler hopped out and strode towards us. He masked his surprise at seeing Floyd and climbed up the stairs to shake his hand and offer condolences.

"Man, it's just crazy," Floyd said. "We had that gig last night—you were there—and we were jamming good. Then she got sick, and Zander took her home. It was the end of the night, and I didn't think too much about it. She could have eaten something that threw her off. Hard to say."

Christie leaned in. "Floyd, was Norah drinking again?"

Floyd shook his head. "Nope. Absolutely not. That girl has been sober for thirty years or more. Stronger than ever. Could be food poisoning?"

"Has anyone else reported food poisoning?" I asked. "When James and I saw her leaving, Zander had to hold her up."

"We offered to help, but—" James started.

"Nah, she would never impose on you like that. Zander—that's another story. They go way back."

We sat in silence for a few minutes; the breeze shuffled the napkins on the table, and the leaves jostled on the branches. Tyler stood up, and Sofia followed him. They unloaded the items from the hardware store and carried them to the back.

"That's my signal to get back to work," James said. "Let me know if I can do anything, Floyd."

Floyd nodded and gave James an appreciative smile. "Thanks, man. Will do."

Meanwhile, Elsi cleared the dishes, leaving us the coffee carafe, and disappeared into the kitchen, leaving Christie and me alone with Floyd. He sighed and buried his head in his hands.

"I'm sorry, Minna. I couldn't think where else to go after I heard the news. I was home when I got the call, and pacing around my house was driving me crazy." He glanced at Christie. "I guess I just needed some friendly faces."

Christie's phone pinged, and I recognized the tone from her dating app. She ignored it. "I'm glad you came. I'm just sorry we weren't here when you arrived."

"Elsi took good care of me," Floyd said, directing his statement at me. "And your daughter, Sofia, is a lovely person. You have a wonderful family."

"I do." Since returning to Lakewood, I appreciated having family nearby and close friends to rely on. In the city, I had friends, but it wasn't the same as living with my mother and daughter, and having Christie and James nearby.

"I didn't want to say this when everyone was around, but—"

"What is it?" Christie asked, alarm written on her face.

"Zander took her home in that state. She was fine until late in the gig. Then she got so sick so fast, but Zander just stepped up and said he'd take her home right away. I just wondered ... I mean, I have my doubts about him."

"You think Zander might have had something to do with Norah's death?" I asked.

"Don't know for sure, but could be. They were friends, but they've always had a rocky relationship ever since they broke up years ago. Love-hate relationship, I'd say." Floyd's jaw tensed, and he pursed his lips. "I don't have any evidence. It's just a hunch."

"A hunch is a good start. Can you connect him to Richard Alcott?" I asked.

"Only Norah. She's the one connecting Zander and Rickie. Rickie wanted to date her, but she'd always refused him. But then

Zander comes along, replaces him as the drummer, and dates the girl he worshipped. Must have been difficult for Rickie back then."

"Hmm." If Floyd couldn't piece it together, what made me think I could?

"My mamma always said the truth will out. It always does. I just hope nobody thinks it was my doing. Norah knew both of them. So did I."

Christie gasped and covered her mouth. "You can't be a suspect. There's no reason for that suspicion."

"No, but people think what they think. People love to pit bandmates against one another for no reason." Floyd shrugged. "Thanks, ladies. I really appreciate the coffee and the chat, and everything. I'm going home to sleep. If I can."

Christie gave him a hug. "Rest, at least. I'll check in on you later." We watched as he made his way down the patio stairs towards the driveway, disappearing around the corner.

"Well, what do you make of that?" I asked.

Christie bit her lip and tapped her fingers on the table. "I don't like this, Minna. I don't like this one bit. Floyd is a gentle soul. He wouldn't harm anyone."

"Why would he be worried about being a suspect?" I asked, not wanting to disagree with her. If I'd learned anything, it was that everyone was a suspect. I picked up the envelope I'd stashed under my coffee cup and gently ripped it open under the seal.

It was a folded note on plain white stationery, written in calligraphy. There was no way for me to recognize the handwriting.

"What is it?" Christie said, alarmed now. My face must have revealed its dark contents.

I passed her the note, and Christie gasped. "This is a threat, Minna." Her eyes widened, and she grabbed my hand, holding it in a death grip.

I gulped and nodded. Someone wanted me to stop investigating the deaths, or I'd be next. The message was simple and effective. But I couldn't stop now.

Chapter 30

The next day, Lillian pushed open the doors to the kitchen and swept in to pour herself a coffee. This wasn't our usual experience with guests, but she had been with us so long, she basically had free rein of the entire house.

"I could have delivered a tray to you, Lillian. You are still our guest," Mom said, already primed for the day. Meanwhile, I slumped in a kitchen chair, trying to get some energy before taking Hugo on a trail walk. Sofia had already gone off to work at Nordic Cozy.

"Nonsense, Elsi darling. I can pour my own coffee. I may be a guest, but I want to make myself useful. No more lolly-gagging about for me. I hope you don't mind I've extended my stay. I really can't imagine leaving Lakewood before learning what happened to dear Richard." Lillian poured herself a mug and sat at the end of the long table, beside my mother.

"Stay as long as you want, Lillian. We're happy to have you," I said.

"Well, as a thank you, I would like to host a dinner here if you don't mind. I've already asked Michael's Catering, and they will provide the food. You don't have to lift a finger." Lillian beamed.

"Tonight?" I tried not to stammer, but I wasn't used to anyone planning events without consulting us. What would Christie say? "I suppose ... that would be lovely, Lillian."

"Wonderful. I will make all the calls. Jack and Grace, Christie, of course. Your family. And that lovely man of yours, James. Do invite him."

"Oh, he's not my—"

"James will be here today to finish the breakfast nook, if I'm not mistaken. Of course we'll ask him," Mom said.

My cheeks burned. "Can we accommodate two more? Christie might like to invite Floyd, and Sofia could invite Tyler."

Lillian clapped her hands. "The more, the merrier! If you think of anyone else, please invite them, too. It's about time we had some levity after everything that's happened here. Bring some positive light into this house."

With that, Lillian whisked herself away, presumably to make plans, leaving Mom and me speechless.

"Well, Hygge House is hosting another dinner. What do you say about that?" Mom asked.

"To be honest, I'm just happy not to plan this one. If Lillian wants to host, she can be my guest." Well, she was my guest, but anyway. I didn't mind her taking over for a night.

That evening, we gathered around the long table in the sunroom. The evening was warm enough to keep the windows open, and candlelight flooded the space. Soft music played in the background, from the seventies, I believed. Elsi and Lillian had probably chosen the music together.

Michael served the meal himself, looking official in his black shirt and dress pants, with a grey pinstriped apron. If nothing else, Michael was a perfectionist, and the meal was spectacular, as usual.

"What do you think of the menu?" Lillian asked as we enjoyed our first few bites. "I asked Michael to prepare a traditional Nordic midsummer meal, and I believe he delivered."

"Spectacular. Well done, you," Mom said after tasting the smoked salmon salad.

"Thank you, Elsi," Michael said, clearly pleased with the compliment.

My first bite of the warm barley salad made me ask for the recipe. Pickled beets and cucumbers, devilled eggs, and a variety of breads made the meal light and summery.

Sofia explained what everything was to Tyler, who looked skeptical at first but seemed to enjoy everything he tried, even helping himself to more.

"It was so nice of you to bring us all together," Grace said, dabbing her lips with her linen napkin. Suddenly I remembered the napkin found near Richard's body, the same colour we had used for the rehearsal dinner. I shuddered.

"Yeah, thanks, Mom," Jack added. "It's been a difficult time."

As Michael cleared away the dinner dishes, Lillian poured everyone another glass of wine. "I'm thrilled you enjoyed it, and it's lovely to see everyone sitting around this table once more." I have to admit, I bristled a little at that statement. It wasn't her table, after all.

Christie coughed into her napkin. Clearly, she was thinking exactly what I was thinking.

"Apart from enjoying a good meal together, thanks to Michael, I wanted to bring you all together. I think I've cracked the case."

I emitted a gasp audible to everyone at the table, but as I surveyed the room, I realized everyone looked astonished. Eyes wide open and jaws practically hitting the table.

"What do you mean, Lillian? You know who killed Uncle Rick?" Jack looked a little terrified.

"Yes," she said, her voice very calm. "I believe I do." Candles flickered and shadows waved across the wall.

James cleared his throat and gazed across the table at me. He took a sip of his wine. I couldn't quite read his expression, but I imagined he was attempting not to roll his eyes.

"Why don't you go ahead? You have us all on pins and needles," I said.

"Yes, well. I'll start by saying definitively that my son, Jack, is not guilty of these murders. He was at the pool hall with Harry on the day Richard was murdered, and then he was at the rehearsal dinner. He had no way of dragging the body to the lakeside. And he was with Grace at the cottage party the whole time. Priya and the bakery ladies can attest to that. There was no way he could have poisoned Norah."

Jack hung his head in embarrassment. If he were guilty, he probably wouldn't want his mom to be talking about the crimes. If he wasn't guilty, he probably didn't want her defending him.

Just then, Michael arrived carrying a vanilla cake with strawberry filling on a pedestal plate.

"Oh my. You've really outdone yourself," Mom said. "This was my husband's favourite cake. I always made it for Vilhelm on his birthday."

My dad loved a strawberry cake with fresh berries, and real whipped cream. Mother's expression made me nostalgic for my childhood and miss my father in that sharp way that comes on so quickly. Perhaps that was how Jack had been feeling about his uncle, who was more like his father than anyone else in his life.

Despite our curiosity about Lillian's theory, we waited as Michael cut pieces and delivered them to everyone at the table. When everyone had settled again, we all turned to Lillian, who had a piece of cake on her fork and was about to take a bite.

Lillian put down her fork and sat straighter, her fingertips touching each other in a loose triangle. "I see you are ready for me to proceed. So, I have established that Jack could not have possibly murdered his uncle or the singer. That leaves the one person who must be guilty. That person is ..."

I leaned in, waiting for her to finish her sentence. It felt like one of those TV reality shows where the host deliberately pauses for dramatic effect, causing the viewer to wonder what he or she will reveal next. Sometimes it's whether the guest will keep their house or sell, and sometimes it's who has won the talent competition. Either way, I wanted answers.

"The drummer." Lillian pronounced her statement with dramatic flair.

"The drummer?" Tyler asked. "You mean Zander Thomsen?" Tyler couldn't hide his tone of disbelief.

"Yes, dear boy. Zander, the drummer. He took Norah home after the cottage party, and the next day she was dead. He was here on the evening of the rehearsal party, and then Richard was dead. Zander took Richard's place in the band. He dated Norah, the very person Richard was interested in dating himself. He *must* be the one."

Lillian sounded so sure she almost convinced me. "Have you spoken to the police about your theory?"

Lillian waved her hand as if to swat at an annoying fly. "Yes, of course. That Detective Whitford said he would consider it, but needed actual evidence. That's where you come in."

"What do you mean?" Christie asked.

Lillian surveyed the table, looking at each of us individually for several seconds. "I'm tasking everyone of you to find the evidence to convict Zander Thomsen of these crimes. He must not go unpunished. And to incentivize you, I'm offering ten thousand dollars to the person who discovers the evidence." From her purse, she took out a wad of bills and shook it at us.

This time, everyone gasped. James shook his head and crossed his arms. "You want to pit us against each other to find evidence against someone, even though we don't know whether he's guilty? That's unethical."

I agreed. "Investigations are about finding out who committed the crime, not manufacturing evidence to convict someone based on a theory." I tried not to sound angry, but I was.

"Lillian, dear. Put away your money. We don't need money to find the guilty party. We need facts." My mother spoke gently to Lillian, touching her arm to get her to sit down.

Lillian slumped into her chair and buried her head in her hands, her shoulders shaking as she sobbed. "I'm sorry. I just can't take it anymore. We can't just go on every day not having answers about what happened to Richard. I loved him."

Jack pushed his chair back and gathered her in his arms. "Everything's going to be okay, Mom."

"To be honest, I've been thinking along the same lines as you, Lillian," I said, hoping to smooth out the uncomfortable situation. "But let's work on finding out who actually killed Norah and Richard, and not pin it on anyone just because he has a motive."

"Agreed," Christie said.

Lillian sat straighter and wiped her nose with the napkin. "Yes, you're right, of course. I just don't believe my son is guilty of these crimes, and Zander is the most likely person I could think of."

"Did Richard talk about those days? You mentioned he was in love with Norah back then." I took a bite of the strawberry cake, trying to keep it casual now that Lillian was calming down.

"Richard told me how much he loved playing in the band. And he was great, too. But he was a loner and felt awkward around the other guys. He had one good friend with whom he spent a lot of time, but he was dating Norah. He once said he hung around that guy just so he could be around Norah." Lillian shook her head. "Young love is very difficult. Everything feels so intense."

Mom nodded. "Yes, I remember how that felt. One's first love is so important, so beautiful." I rolled my eyes as if I were a teenager. I didn't really want to hear about my mother's first love.

Christie grinned at my reaction, and I kicked her under the table.

"Who was Richard's friend back then? I'm guessing it was Floyd or Jed."

"No, Minna. He admired Floyd, and they were friendly. Same with Jed. But he spent a lot of time outside rehearsals with Reggie," Lillian said. She gazed into her wineglass as if the memories were there in the depths of the crystal.

"Isn't Reggie the guy who was playing on Saturday night at the cottage?" Christie turned to Tyler.

"Yeah, that's him. He doesn't play with them all the time, but once in a while, I guess." Tyler shifted uncomfortably as all eyes turned on him.

"That doesn't mean he would hurt Richard or Norah though, does it?" Sofia asked, her voice soft.

"No, it just means they were all in the same band around the same time. Means nothing," James replied.

Lillian stood up. "I'm very sorry. I do hope we find the actual killer. Poor Norah. And my dear Richard." Lillian stifled a sob, and Jack guided her out of the room, looking disappointed and embarrassed.

Grace stood up and said it was time to go, so I accompanied her to the front door. "I'm sorry about all this," Grace said. "She can't deal with her grief, and she's imagining every possibility. I was the same when Owen died."

I squeezed Grace's hand. "Don't worry. Whether it's Zander or someone else, they won't get away with it."

Grace nodded and smiled. "She's right about one thing, though. Jack is not guilty of these crimes. He loved his Uncle Rick too much, and he didn't even know Norah."

Just then, Jack returned. We said goodnight on the porch, and I watched Grace drive away with her husband. I hoped she was right for the sake of her family. She didn't need another devastating loss.

And James was probably right about Zander and Reggie, but it didn't hurt to learn a little more about their connections to Richard and Norah. James's father, Henri, could help. After all, he knew where Reggie lived and had even worked on the old house.

Chapter 31

The next afternoon, James and I poured over the drawings for the attic, laid out on the table in the Aurora Room. It was my favourite space to work these days, not only because of the good-sized workspace, but also the library feel and the natural light flooding in. Hugo lay in his doggie bed nearby, occasionally twitching as if he were running after something.

Now that the breakfast nook was done, Christie and I decided the unused attic space needed to be tackled because it was, as she said, useless space and lost revenue. The attic was currently a wide-open space with large windows at either end and plenty of ceiling height. We had discussed creating several individual bedrooms upstairs to accommodate more guests.

"Listen, Minna. You have so much space up there that you could do one large bedroom with a living room, a small kitchenette area and ensuite and still have room for two additional bedrooms with their own bathrooms." James pointed at his drawings.

"I love it, but we need to consult with Christie," I said, imagining how I could design these spaces to maximize the light and account for the sloped ceilings.

Just then, Sofia rushed in, cellphone in hand. Breathless, she paused by the table and held out her phone. Hugo jumped out of his doggie bed and rushed towards her, pawing at her legs to get her attention.

"What is it?" I asked. Usually she was showing me some funny video or meme, but this time I didn't understand what she wanted me to look at.

"Just scroll," she said, leaning down to scratch Hugo behind the ears.

I took the phone from her hand and scrolled down the feed, noting images of Paris at twilight, the Louvre bouncing sunshine from its peaks, and the Eiffel Tower lit up at night. "Great photos," I said, returning Sofia's phone.

Sofia sighed. "No, Mom. Look closely. This is Eloise's social media feed."

"Okay," I replied, scrolling to the top to see Eloise wearing a wide-brimmed hat and noticing the enormous social media following she had. "What am I looking at?"

"Keep scrolling until you see Hygge House."

Christie leaned over my shoulder as I scrolled past the Paris photos, to the train station, the airport, videos from inside an airplane. "Wow, she really made Hygge House look amazing."

"This is a good selfie of Norah and Eloise at the wedding," I said, admiring the two women. "They kind of look alike, don't they?"

"Check out the one by the shoreline," Sofia said. She reached over and started scrolling for me. I watched the images whiz by.

She stopped when she found the one she wanted: a shot of an empty Muskoka chair facing the lake. The same chair where we found Richard Alcott's body. "When was this taken?" I asked. I turned the phone so James and Christie could see it more clearly.

"Keep going, Mom. There's more." Sofia's eyebrows furrowed together, and she squished her fingers the way she often did when concentrating or nervous.

"Oh! Stop there," Christie said.

I zoomed in closer on a photo taken at dusk of the landscape from my mother's garden, looking out toward the lake. At first glance, the photo was serene, with the sun setting in the west, providing only a glimmer of light at the edge of the photo. It was the dark shadow that intrigued me.

"Who is that?" I asked. The figure appeared to be a man, but I recognized nothing about him. "That's not you, is it?"

James looked closely and shook his head. "Nope, not me. I don't recognize him. Maybe a wedding guest? Someone at the rehearsal party?"

"Eloise took photos of everything before, during, and after the wedding. There may be more clues in her social media feed or in the photos she didn't post," Sofia said. "If the killer was at the rehearsal or at the wedding, we should see some kind of suspicious activity, right?"

"Brilliant, Sofia. Can you get in touch and ask Eloise to send us all the photos?" I asked. Why hadn't I thought of that earlier?

"Already done. She said she'd send them right over. But there are a lot of photos, so it might take some time. Do you think there's something here?" Sofia took her phone back and scrolled through the photos.

"I hope so. The man in the dark gives me the shivers. We might link the photo to Richard's death if we can figure out when it was taken. It's such a strange place for anyone to be walking. There are no paths or trails there. It's kind of out of the way."

Sofia crossed her legs. Within a few moments, Freya emerged from her hiding place and jumped onto her lap, nuzzling Sofia until she got attention. As usual, Astrid stayed curled up in the distance, ignoring us all.

"Sounds like a good time to take a break," Christie said. "I'll get the coffee, but yell if Eloise's text comes in."

James and I sat on the couch, facing the fireplace. "Remind me again. What are your current theories?"

"Well, we can rule out natural causes for Richard and Norah, and it's clear Richard didn't take his own life. Lise Tremblay said it was almost impossible." I pulled a pillow onto my lap.

Sofia nodded. "What about Lillian Alcott?"

"I've been thinking a lot about her. She married Jack's father, Patrick, and after he died, she got involved with Richard, but didn't make it public. Even Jack didn't realize how they felt about each other. That's a long time to keep it a secret."

"And she encouraged him to come to Lakewood. Would she lure him here only to kill him at her son's wedding? And why would she kill Norah? Rick and Norah never even had a relationship." James crossed his arms. "Would Lillian be jealous of a girlfriend Rick never had?"

"Good question. And then there are the bandmates. Norah, of course, is no longer a suspect. But what about Floyd, Jed, and Zander? What reason would they have to go after Richard or Norah?" Hugo jumped onto the couch and settled between James and me. No worries in the world.

"Anyone else who was at the wedding?" Sofia asked. "Jack's brother Ian, sister-in-law Kate, and their daughter Rosie. Pastor Dahl, Harry and Eloise, plus some locals who are friends of Jack and Grace." Sofia appeared perplexed. "I just don't get it."

Sofia's phone pinged. "It's Eloise. She's given me a link to a photo file." With flying fingers, Sofia texted back.

"Why don't we look at them on your computer screen?" James asked, making his way to the table where I'd set up my laptop earlier in the day.

Sofia shared the link, and before long we gathered around my laptop, looking at each photo one by one. Most of them were just beautiful shots of Grace and Jack and the wedding party, flowers in the garden, or selfies of Eloise. Now and again, we focussed more closely.

"Look there," I said. "This is the man we saw earlier." We paused on the next two photos, variations of the same. "Stop there, Sofia. He's not alone."

Sofia zoomed in. Walking behind the figure was another, smaller person, possibly a younger person or a woman, moving away from the Muskoka chair. The closer we moved in, the grainier the photo became, what with the dull lighting and distance.

"Let's presume these are the people who dragged Richard to the Muskoka chair, drugged or already dead. They used the rake to cover their tracks and the distraction of the rehearsal dinner to dump the body. If there were two, one could have driven Richard's car to the house, and the other driven the getaway car."

"Makes more sense than one person doing it alone. But who are they?" Sofia asked.

Christie returned with coffee. "Hey, you were supposed to tell me when the photos came in."

"Sorry," I said. "We got so excited we forgot. But check this out." Christie put down the tray and peered over Sofia's shoulder at the photo we'd examined. "Do you think that's Norah with him?"

"Could be. But why would the person kill her afterward?" I poured another cup of coffee. I needed more caffeine to straighten out my swirling ideas.

"If Norah was involved in what happened, the murderer may have got rid of her, too," Christie said.

I looked more closely at the photograph. The smaller figure could indeed be Norah. We spent the next few hours searching through the photographs, but eventually Christie had to leave for an appointment, and Sofia to meet Tyler. That left James and me alone, both too tired to look at the drawings for the attic and frustrated by searching through the photos.

Instead, I lit the fireplace, and we sat on the couch enjoying each other's quiet company as we both—I'm guessing—contemplated the murders.

Chapter 32

Boreal and Beanery was quiet for a weekday morning, and Christie and I practically had the place to ourselves. I'd left Tuuli parked outside Nordic Cozy, and Hugo was spending some time in the store with Sofia, giving me a chance to give all my attention to Christie as we waited for Grace and Jack to join us.

"Are you doing okay?" I asked, reaching out to touch her hand.

Christie's skin was pale, and her usual vibrancy had disappeared. "I will be. I'm having difficulty sleeping. I keep having weird dreams, as though I'm drowning and trying to fight my way to shore."

"It doesn't surprise me, what with everything that's happening. It feels like we're drowning in bad news. Plus, our business ..." I shook my head.

The bell over the door rang, and both of us looked up, expecting the newlyweds. In fact, it was another couple. Reggie White held the door open for a woman. I scoured my memory, barely able to place her, and then I remembered.

"That's the desk clerk from Driftwood Cottages," I whispered. "She's the one who was working during the rehearsal dinner and wouldn't tell me anything about Richard checking in. I mean, I get it, privacy and all that, but you'd think she'd at least check if he was in for me."

Reggie glanced our way but averted his eyes. Was he trying not to notice us? Or did he not register who we were? He and

Stella placed their orders with Sarah and took their coffee to go. I couldn't help but track them as they left the coffee shop and jumped into his beat-up old truck across the street.

"Just a sec. I'll be right back," I said, ambling over to the front counter. "Do you recognize those two?" I asked Sarah.

"Nah. Not really," Sarah said. "They come in once in a while, grab their coffee, but they never stay. I haven't really chatted with them much. He lives out in the boonies in some old cottage. A bit of a loner, I'd say."

"That's what Henri said. And she's his—"

Sarah shrugged. "Partner, I guess? Girlfriend? Neither is wearing a ring. What's your interest in them, Minna?"

"I'm not sure yet," I said. "I just have this feeling that I can't quite explain."

"Like spidey senses?" Sarah laughed. "Christie warned me about your hunches. I thought you were never wrong."

"Not so sure about that. I've been wrong plenty of times, but I am learning to listen to my gut. Thanks, Sarah."

"Yeah, no worries," she said.

I returned to the table where Christie was examining the printouts I'd made of some of Eloise's photographs. I pointed at the man and woman partially obscured by the shadows in the landscape. "Look familiar?"

She shook her head and sighed. "I mean, it could be anyone. Zander and Norah. Floyd and Eloise. James and you. Heck, even Reggie and Stella," she said, motioning outside to where the couple had been.

Defeated, I slouched in my chair and sipped my chai latte. "Yeah, you're right. I have a nagging feeling that the murders have something to do with that band. They're all so connect-ed."

A few minutes later, Jack and Grace arrived. They gave us a little wave before ordering their coffee and heading toward our table.

"Hello there, newlyweds," Christie said, putting on her brightest smile. "So good to see you both." I admired how she could turn it on when she needed to.

Both smiled at us in greeting, but the dark circles under Jack's eyes told a different story. We chit-chatted for a bit, but I could tell Grace wanted to get to the real reason we'd invited them for coffee.

"Right. Eloise was kind enough to share all the images from your rehearsal party and wedding, including the ones she didn't share online. Have you seen the photos?" I asked.

Grace shook her head. "No, she just sent me a curated list of photographs—the best ones, she said—and even those were a lot. I've glanced at them, but I haven't really had time to look them over closely."

I glanced at Christie, who nodded. "The thing is, we think Eloise captured some images, and we wanted you to identify if they're guests."

I handed over the printout of the photograph we'd been most interested in and watched their reactions. "Were they at the rehearsal party?"

Grace shook her head. "No, I don't think so. They don't look like any family members or friends of ours. It's hard to tell with their obscured faces, and I can't even tell what they're wearing."

"What about you, Jack?" Christie asked.

"Same here. I don't recognize them, but they could be any-one, really. Do you think they're responsible for Uncle Rick's death?"

"Not sure," I said. "Thanks to Eloise, we have something to go on, at least."

The colour rose in Grace's cheeks, and she stared at her hands cupping her coffee mug. "It may not be my place to tell you this, but I want to in case … I mean, I don't think it has anything to do with …"

"Go ahead, Gracie. Tell them," Jack said in his gentlest tone.

"The whole time Eloise was here, she kept asking when she could meet Norah Kincaid. Then, when the rehearsal came, she was obsessed. I thought at first she was a fan of the band, but that wasn't it at all."

"Eloise took a lot of selfies with Norah. They seemed to hit it off," Christie said.

Grace clutched her hands in her lap. "When Eloise returned to Paris, she wrote me a long text, and what she said shocked me. I knew Eloise had adoptive parents, but she didn't know who her biological parents were. Apparently, she's been trying to find her mother for years. She did the whole DNA testing and everything."

I was on the edge of my seat now, scrambling all the scattered pieces together in my mind to form the puzzle. "No. It can't be. Norah is Eloise's biological mother?"

Grace nodded, her eyebrows raised. "Right? It surprised me, too."

"And Eloise told Norah at the wedding?" Christie asked. "That's why she was so obsessed with her."

"No, Eloise just wanted to get to meet her, see what she was like first. Before she boarded the plane, she messaged Norah to tell her the truth. Apparently, Norah had thought she was just a clingy fangirl. They planned to get together this summer in Paris. And now ..." Grace stifled a sniffle, the tears forming in her eyes.

Jack placed an arm over Grace's shoulder.

"I'm sorry. It was important for Eloise to find her mother. And then she does, and she's taken away so soon."

My mind was spinning. Eloise was Norah's daughter, but she gave her up at birth. "Does Eloise know who her father is?"

"She hoped Norah would tell her, but she kept that part a secret. Eloise isn't even sure if her father ever knew about her birth." Grace shuddered. "Can you imagine not knowing where you came from?"

"No, I can't." I was so grateful for the good relationships I had with my mother, Elsi, and Sofia. I couldn't imagine not having either of them in my life. My heart went out to Eloise.

"It wasn't really my place to tell you. I should have left it to Eloise, but I was worried. Someone killed Uncle Rick, and then Norah died. What if it has something to do with Eloise and her search for her parents?" Grace wiped tears from her eyes.

"You did the right thing," I said. "Eloise will understand that we're trying to help solve these crimes."

As Jack and Grace made to leave, Christie reached over and took Grace's hand. "Tell us if there is anything we can do," she said.

"Find who did this," she said. "For Jack. And for Eloise."

The bell above the door chimed as they exited, and I felt the tension in my shoulders, as if they were up to my ears, and attempted to relax. "That was not what I expected."

"Do you think one of her bandmates is the father?" Christie asked, her eyes widening.

"Definitely not Floyd. He and Norah didn't have that kind of relationship. But she seems to have dated almost everyone else. Reggie and Zander to start. But apparently, not Richard. Unless that's a secret she kept, too. Worthwhile having a few conversations," I said.

Christie agreed and smiled.

I gave her a quizzical look, and she shrugged, taking a sip of her chai latte. "It's like that quaint little village Miss Marple lived in, teeming with secrets."

"Ah yes, but secrets get revealed, don't they?" To which we clinked our mugs.

Chapter 33

A few hours later, I held Tuuli's handlebars and encouraged Hugo to hop out of the trailer. "Not this time, buddy. I have to do this alone."

Hugo barked, but jumped out and sat at my feet.

"Are you sure about this, Minna?" Christie asked, a worried expression crossing her face.

"Yes, of course. You have Mom's book club meeting to prepare for. It wouldn't look good if neither of us was there. Besides, I'll be back in no time." I put on my most reassuring smile and waved my hand like breaking into someone's house was no big deal. I mean, I'd broken into Richard's rental cottage. Nothing happened then.

"Okay, but keep your cellphone on you the whole time. Be quick."

I agreed and pushed off, pedalling toward the boardwalk. My mother had always said I was too impetuous. When I got an idea in my head, I couldn't ignore it. She was still right.

Zander's bungalow was at the end of Birch Street, close to Driftwood Cottages. The boardwalk brought me to the cottage area, and I turned onto Lakeshore Drive before heading up Birch Street. Mom had mentioned he'd bought his parents' house when they moved to Florida a few years earlier. From the outside, the red-brick house looked tidy, but could use some updates. Zander didn't seem the type to care much about current trends, though.

I parked Tuuli on the sidewalk, trying to appear confident, but my knees shook and my breath was shallow. I knocked on the door, loud enough to let him know I was here, but not aggressively. No one answered.

Nothing was visible through the 1970s-style teardrop window. I glanced around me, but no one was in sight. Like the last time I broke into a place, I took out my credit card and a hairpin, but before I attempted my new trick, I tried the handle. Lo-and-behold, the door opened.

Without hesitation, I stepped inside and called out. "Zander? Are you home?"

Hearing nothing, I stepped into the living room, its bay window facing the street side. The house looked as though it was straight out of my early childhood with orange shag rug, upholstered furniture, and brick fireplace. To be fair, it was well-preserved, but felt a lot like walking into a museum, or at least a recreated set for a television show. I shuddered to think that the bungalow had replaced one of the more beautiful heritage houses that had stood here before a fire ravaged this part of town.

As I moved through the room, I scanned for anything of interest. On the pedestal table beside the couch, I found a few sci-fi books. A bookmark from Saga and Stone Bookstore—currently up for sale—peeked out from a recent thriller. A newer television seemed too modern to hang over the fireplace. The remote and a laptop sat on the coffee table beside a set of coasters, sitting in the middle. Zander was a neat freak.

I headed to the kitchen. The green appliances against the yellow tiles were even more retro than the living room. On the kitchen table, surrounded by four spindle chairs, I found a basket filled with bills, stationery, and pens. I rifled through. At the bottom, I found it. A Schaeffer pen, the same kind that was likely used to write Richard's note and the death threat I'd received.

Just then, the back door opened, and I froze. How foolish of me not to have checked the backyard before deciding Zander wasn't home. His footsteps came towards me, and I had to decide. Stay and face him or run out of the house, knowing he would see me. I stayed.

"Oh, Zander. Just who I was looking for," I said, standing awkwardly beside the kitchen table. I crossed my arms to hide the pen from his sight.

Zander's eyebrows knitted together. "Minna? What are you doing here?" he asked, not unkindly.

"I came over, frankly, because I had some questions for you. The door was open, and no one answered when I called—"

"So you let yourself in?" Zander frowned. "What's going on?"

"Yeah, sorry about that. I don't normally enter places without being invited. Well, the thing is, you were close to Norah. You were in a relationship with her for a long time—"

"Hang on. What does that have to do with you?" Zander pulled out his cellphone.

"Did you know she had a child? Did she tell you she adopted it out?" I asked, feeling a sudden gut-wrenching knot in my stomach. Who was I to share this news? It was Norah's secret to tell. Or Eloise's.

Zander shook his head. "No, Norah never told me about that. What does it have to do with me?"

"I don't know. The girl—she's a grown woman now—would be in her early thirties. I'm guessing she had her about the time she got clean." Would Zander remember that time?

He lowered himself into a chair, appearing haggard. "Yeah, I remember she went away for a while back then. She came back a changed person. Never touched another drop. But a baby? I didn't know."

"I take it you and Richard Alcott weren't close. Norah once said you two weren't friendly." I sat in the chair opposite, careful not to make any sudden moves in case I spooked him.

"We didn't know each other well enough to like or dislike each other. Rick resented my taking his place as the drummer. He made that clear. And Jed told me later he was upset when I started dating Norah, but we never fought about it. Rick had moved away by then."

"Did you visit Rick on the night of the rehearsal party? In his cottage at Driftwood?"

"No. I was with the band. In fact, we were at Hygge House setting up for the rehearsal dinner." Zander's expression changed from concern to anger. "Are you trying to pin these deaths on me? Just because Rick and I didn't get along doesn't mean I'd kill the guy! And Norah ... I loved her. We just couldn't make it work."

"You didn't write a note using this pen? A goodbye note? Planted it in Rick's cottage?"

"What? No! You're crazy, lady." Zander pushed his chair back and stood up. "I'm going to ask you to leave now," he said. "The police are on their way."

Really? Zander was calling the police on me. I took a deep breath. "Zander, this is about finding who did it. We need answers. Jack needs them. And so does Eloise, Norah's daughter."

Zander's jaw dropped. "The maid of honour was Norah's daughter?" Now, he looked genuinely shocked.

"Is there something you're not telling me?" I asked in a gentle tone.

"Okay, I'll admit I was at the Driftwood Cottages before coming to your place. I had a whiskey and a smoke with Rick. Truthfully, he didn't want to come to town, and I thought it was because of me. I wanted to bury the hatchet. We had a good chat, and I left feeling better about it. Turns out it had nothing to do with me."

"What did it have to do with?" I asked. The pieces were coming together, if only in a jagged pattern.

"He didn't explain. Something about the past and not wanting to dredge it up again," Zander said. "But I didn't kill the man. And I certainly didn't murder Norah. I loved her."

The door swung open, and Detective Whitford entered. "Ah, Minna. Now I get it. Why am I not surprised?"

I shrugged and smiled. "We just like to meet on the best occasions, I guess. Zander and I were talking about Norah."

"And Richard Alcott?" Whitford raised his eyebrows and tilted his head. "Everything okay here, Zander?"

Zander nodded. "Yeah, it's fine. I panicked a little when I found her in the house."

"You know, you could have a restraining order placed against Ms. Halonen," Whitford said, a sly smile spreading across his face. I wasn't entirely sure if he was serious.

"No, it's fine," Zander said. He rubbed his forehead with his fingers.

"Besides, I was just leaving," I added. "I appreciate your frankness, Zander. If there's anything else, please get in touch."

Whitford opened the door for me. "You're not investigating, are you, Minna?"

"Just having a chat with Zander. Giving my condolences," I said. I didn't like to lie, but somehow old patterns die hard. It wasn't the first time I'd stretched the truth with Detective Whitford. He'd known me for too many decades, and could probably tell I wasn't being 100 percent truthful.

"Have yourself a fine day, now," Whitford said, closing the door behind me.

I practically jogged over to Tuuli and pedalled away, trying not to look like a criminal and more like a middle-aged woman on a pleasant cycle. I felt like an old fool confronting Zander when I'd had no reason to suspect him, except a hunch. Whitford was right. I should just stay out of it.

Chapter 34

Dust flew up and scattered in the air, sunlight from the small window illuminating it as it drifted and settled. I sneezed and then sneezed again.

"Sorry about that," I said, dropping the sheet onto the plank floor. "Should have thought about the dust going everywhere."

"Occupational hazard, I'm afraid. Let's see what we have here." James removed his hat and ran his fingers through his hair, surveying the furniture. "It's in remarkably good condition."

"We can definitely use some of it here, but I'll probably store the rest for the time being while we decide. And I'm sure Dev can sell a few pieces for me at Vintage Pier." I leaned against a highboy and tried to see past the clutter.

"Okay, I'll get Tyler in one day next week, and we can move the furniture out of here and into storage. What's the timeline for this project? And the budget?"

"I was waiting for you to ask—"

Sounds in the stairwell stopped me cold. "What was that?"

James shook his head. "Sounded like footsteps, but could be something between the walls or in the ceiling."

"Please, no animals in the walls." The price you paid for living near nature, Henri had said. He was right, but I didn't want to deal with renovations and animals.

We stood still, listening for more sounds. Then they started again. Distinct footsteps from the stairwell. Was Fanny finally making her presence known to me? Mom still claimed she had conversations with the lady. I didn't buy it, but now I had my doubts.

James grabbed a poker from an old fireplace set and positioned himself near the top of the stairs. I trailed behind him at a safe distance. He raised the poker as if it were a baseball bat.

In the doorway, a figure appeared. It gasped.

I exhaled, and James let the poker down. Floyd raised a hand to his chest, his breath heavy. "You startled me," he said, then grinned. "I'm not in such great shape anymore. Had to take a breather partway up."

"We thought you were—" I started. "Well, we didn't know who was coming up the stairs."

"Sorry, pal. Didn't mean to shock you," James said, returning the poker to the set. "What brings you up to the rafters?"

Floyd took a seat on an old milk crate, his breath easing now. "Found Elsi fussing in the garden. She was kind enough to tell me where you two were. Those are some steep steps, I must say."

"We figure it was the servants' staircase, back in the day. We plan to join the second floor to the attic with a new set of stairs at the front of the house." James showed him our initial plans on the drawings we'd had drawn up.

After a brief discussion of our attic remodel, Floyd crossed his arms and hung his head. "I'm sorry to come here like this, but I just had a mind it was my responsibility. I take care of my band. When there's trouble, I'm there for them."

I nodded. "Is this about my visit to Zander's house?"

"No, not exactly. He told me you, um, stopped by and that he, well, called the police." Floyd shuffled from foot to foot. "Totally unnecessary, he said. He seemed apologetic."

"Well, to be fair, I was in his house without permission." Breaking into people's houses wasn't the best idea after all. Not even if I were looking for clues.

"The thing is, I didn't tell you because it wasn't my business. I don't want to spread rumours, you see."

If I were sitting in a chair, I'd be on the edge of my seat. Instead, I casually leaned against a pillar, waiting for Floyd to continue.

"All those years ago, Rickie had a thing for Norah. We all knew. She did too. But she was dating Reggie. The three of them hung out all the time, right through high school and into their early twenties," Floyd said. "Until one night. I was in my garage, playing some music, and Norah rushed in, crying and carrying on. I asked her what happened, but she just shook her head and said she never wanted to see him again."

"Did she mean Richard?" I asked. Did Norah's rift with Richard go back all those decades?

Floyd shook his head. "She was so distraught and wouldn't tell me anything more. Just cried and cried. I did what I could, but she never told me the entire story. That same week, Reggie quit the band, and a few weeks later he drove himself out to Alberta. And Rickie moved to Toronto at the end of the summer."

"Hmm. So something happened that night between the three of them. And no one ever talked about it? Not Reggie? Or Norah?"

"Nope. I asked once, years later, but Reggie said better kept in the past. And Norah refused to talk about it, so I never asked again. Norah started dating Zander soon after she broke up with Reggie, almost like a statement that she wasn't his anymore. Not even sure she liked him all that much, but they got along, so that was enough for her. On and off for years, right 'til the end."

"And Zander doesn't know what happened that night either?"

"I doubt it. Norah could keep a secret, that's for damned sure. And now I'm worried about what happened. Keeps me up at night wondering why someone killed Rickie and then Norah."

I nodded and touched Floyd's arm. "It's been keeping me up, too. Did Reggie ever move on from Norah?"

"Never married, if that's what you mean. She didn't either, for that matter. But he's lived with a woman for at least a decade, or more, out at the old shack. Keep to themselves mostly, but you'll see them in town from time to time. Stella works over at Driftwood Cottages, and Reggie still likes to play some."

"Stella?" I remembered the woman with the dark red lipstick at the front desk, so uninterested in helping me with Richard's disappearance.

"You know her?" Floyd asked.

"Not exactly. I met her once," I said, not wanting to reveal the fact that I'd also broken into Crow's Nest. Floyd might think I was the criminal. "I appreciate you telling us, Floyd."

"Do you think it'll help solve the case?" Floyd's downcast face was the saddest I'd ever seen it. "I don't want anyone to get into trouble, but this is serious stuff. Whoever killed them needs to atone for their crimes."

I'm not much of a hugger, but I threw my arms around Floyd and gave him a bear hug. "We'll do our best. You did the right thing."

When I released him, Floyd wiped away some tears and put on a smile. "I'm off, then," he said. "Wonder if the lady I saw on the stairs will still be there. I said hello, and she just vanished."

James and I exchanged looks. "A lady on the staircase?" Had my mother been right all along?

Floyd laughed. "You have a spirit living here. Not the first one I've seen in Lakewood. Probably not the last."

Floyd left us, the dust settling on the furniture, and we regrouped by looking over the blueprint, but Floyd's memory of that night haunted me. There had to be something more to it.

Chapter 35

The next morning, I sipped a cup of coffee at the lake, sitting in a Muskoka chair. Not *the* Muskoka chair, but another one a fair distance away. Hugo sat at my side, watching a duck and her ducklings paddle near the shore. When I finished my last sip, I stood up and stretched.

"We can't put it off any longer, Hugo," I said. "We need answers." I'd barely slept the night before, mulling over everything Floyd had told us. My instinct was to visit Reggie, but first, I wanted to see Stella.

After dropping off my coffee mug in the kitchen, with Hugo at my heels, I turned back to the garden shed where Tuuli waited patiently.

"On your way out?" Mom asked, squinting against the sun. She raised her hand to shield her eyes, despite the large-brimmed hat. In her other hand, she had a pair of secateurs.

"Shouldn't be long," I said, encouraging Hugo to jump into his doggie trailer.

"Are you headed to town?" she asked. My mom loved to know everything about everyone, but this time, I didn't want to worry her.

"Just going for a ride up the boardwalk and maybe drop by the store to see Sofia. Need anything?" I asked, trying to sound as relaxed as possible, despite my growing trepidation about seeing Stella again. Based on our first interaction, I might not be welcome.

"No, I'm just fine. Cheerio," she said, but she was definitely curious. Despite my age, I still felt like her little girl, sneaking out to create mischief with Christie.

I waved and pushed Tuuli away from the garden shed, hopping on when the ground was more level and we reached the boardwalk. By bicycle, Driftwood Cottages was several kilometres away along the shoreline, but it was the perfect morning for taking the old girl for a spin. And the bike, too.

By the time I passed the Harbour Centre and the Fish 'n' Chips shop, sweat was dripping from my forehead and down my back. Waiting for summer to arrive was a pastime everyone around town had, but once it actually arrived, I remembered how overheated I could become, especially paired with hot flashes. I paused in the park and took a drink of water, giving some to Hugo, who was more pleased than I was to be in the fresh air.

This might not be a good idea after all. I glanced at the tourists taking pictures of the freshly painted gazebo overlooking the lake and smiled at a young woman taking selfies. She reminded me of Eloise. I still had so many questions, but Stella could answer some of them for me.

Back on the bike, feeling refreshed from the water and the breeze coming off the lake, I pushed through the last few kilometres. There was the familiar road leading to the parking area I'd last seen the night we found Richard Alcott's body. The night I saw his note and took a picture.

I left Tuuli parked at a bike rack and put Hugo on a leash. We trekked from the car park to the main lodge. The place looked cheerful in the mid-morning summer light, instead of ghostly like the night Christie and I had broken in.

In the lodge, the scent of bacon and eggs wafted toward me. The breakfast buffet must be in full swing by now. At the front desk, a young woman with long blonde hair looked up and smiled.

"Good morning. Are you checking in?"

"Um, no. I'm actually here to see Stella."

The girl appeared puzzled. "Is she a guest?"

"No, she is a receptionist here." Perhaps this girl was new. She seemed young, so it might be her summer job.

The girl shrugged. The name on her tag said Erin. "Just a second. I'll ask."

Erin popped her head into the backroom, and I heard her muffled question about Stella. A moment later, an older woman appeared, straightening her blouse and skirt.

"You're looking for Stella?" The woman asked. Desk clerks always had a way of both welcoming me and putting me on edge. "If you see her, tell her she can pick up her last paycheque."

"She quit? When?"

"Not exactly." The woman leaned forward against the tall desk and glanced around. Erin had returned to her paperwork, but she appeared as curious as I was about Stella's whereabouts. "Stella just stopped coming to work. Right after the murder. Well, that's not entirely true. Right after that singer died. Didn't answer my calls. No request for a leave of absence. No letter of resignation. We hired this one for the summer," she nodded toward Erin, "but Stella was a full-time employee. We'll need to replace her soon. But after this stunt, Stella is as good as fired."

"Where can I find her?" I asked, my head buzzing with thoughts about the timing.

The woman shrugged. "Beats me. She sometimes lived with her elderly mother in Birchtown, and sometimes with her boyfriend out in the bush. I can't say I knew her too well, to be honest. She was an odd duck."

Before I turned to leave, I paused. "One last question. Was Stella a smoker?"

The woman scoffed. "That girl spent more time on smoke breaks than she did working, I reckon. I told her those things weren't any good for her, but she said they helped her relax. Come to think of it, she was more anxious than usual in the last few days I saw her, but she never said why."

I thanked both of them and headed back out, Hugo at my side. Now what? I could try to find out where her mother lived in Birchtown, but Reggie's property was closer, and she might very well be there. The idea of going there alone made me nervous. Better to ask Christie or James to come with me. Just in case.

Hugo and I jumped back on our ride and headed home. This time, it felt like it took no time to get to Hygge House, probably because my imagination was exploding with scenarios. Stella had left her job, telling no one. The timing seemed too coincidental. I parked Tuuli beside the garden shed and wandered into the house, barely registering the furniture Tyler and James were transporting down the stairs to his truck.

Chapter 36

The drive to Reggie's house—Old Jackson's cabin, as some locals called it—was on a long and narrow unpaved road leading away from town and its amenities. My sedan felt every bump and rut, and Christie held on to the passenger-side handle above her door as if her life depended on it.

"This is why Reggie drives that old, banged-up truck," Christie said. "Your car might not make it out of here alive." She snorted and gave me a wild look.

"Sure is pretty out here, though." I admired the towering trees overhanging the road. "I get why he lives out here in the bush. So private."

"Yeah, so he can bury the bodies." Christie laughed out loud, and I joined in, but I hadn't told her the complete truth. My suspicions about Reggie's behaviour were strong. Had he murdered his ex-girlfriend and his former friend? I was determined to find out.

After several minutes, the road turned into a clearing, with a small house, a shed, and an old barn that was nearly falling apart.

"Wow. This place is from another era," Christie said.

"Henri mentioned Reggie's been working on it, but there's still a lot to do. New roof, though," I said, pointing to the metal shingles. No sign of Reggie's truck, or any other vehicle, for that matter. "Doesn't look like anyone's home." I'd already entered two properties without permission. Was the third time a charm?

Christie paused by her passenger-side door. "Do you think this is a good idea? I mean, if anything happens, our only way out is by car."

I hesitated. She wasn't wrong. "I have an idea. You take my keys and keep the engine running. I'll knock and see if anyone's home, take a quick peek inside. If anything goes wrong, I'll come right back to the car and you gun it." I must have had a smirk on my face because Christie grinned.

"This feels like an episode of *Charlie's Angels*, without Boz. Be careful," she said, taking my keys and getting into the car. I'd left it facing the road for a quick exit.

Despite our banter, Christie was nervous. So was I. Taking a deep breath in, I surveyed the property for signs of the residents, straightened my posture, and strode toward the front porch, avoiding a broken step.

The storm door's fly screen sagged from its frame. I opened it and knocked on the main door, holding my breath, my heart beating against my chest.

"Who's there?" A woman's voice called from inside.

"Stella? It's Minna Halonen from Hygge House. Do you have a minute to chat?" Stella likely knew who I was, not from having talked to her at Driftwood Cottages, but because of Hygge House's connection to at least two of the past three murders in Lakewood.

The door inched open. Stella peered out at me with her unmistakable kohl-lined eyes and signature red lipstick. "What do you want?"

"Do you mind if I come in? I have a few questions, and I think you're the person to ask."

"Not on your life, lady. You can stay right where you are."

"Would you mind coming out for a few minutes? We can talk on the porch." I moved back from the door, giving her lots of space.

Stella hesitated, then pulled the door wider and pushed open the storm door, standing solidly in the doorframe. She looked me up and down, a frown on her face. "I remember you. You were at Driftwood the night Rickie died. You own that big old place near the lake." She took out a pack of cigarettes and lit one.

"Yeah, that's me." I glanced behind her into the living room of the small shack. A television was on, playing some game show or other. "Is Reggie home?"

Stella glared. "What do you want with him? He hasn't been here for days."

"I just had a few questions. I understand Reggie dated Norah back in the day. And was friends with Richard Alcott."

"Yeah. So? That don't make him no murderer," Stella said. She inhaled deeply and blew the smoke in my direction.

I leaned against a pillar, then thought better of it. My weight alone might make the roof collapse on this whole place. "You're right. I'm not accusing him of anything. I just wondered if you ... Did you know Norah had a daughter? Named Eloise?"

A confused expression crossed her face. "A daughter? Like a kid?"

"In her early thirties. She grew up in Lakewood, but with adoptive parents. Norah gave her up when she was born." Stella's reaction suggested this was the first time she'd heard of Norah's child.

"Reggie never told me about no kid. Besides, they weren't together then. After they broke up, Norah wanted nothing to do with him." Stella moved to close the door and end our conversation. "Even when he plays with the band, she barely says two words to him."

"You don't think Eloise is Reggie's, do you?" I asked in my gentlest voice. "Is there anything else Reggie's not telling you? The thing is, I think Reggie has gotten himself into some trouble, and I want to help."

Stella's big brown eyes stared into mine, and I imagined there was sadness there, but as quickly as I registered her pain, she grabbed something from behind the door and pushed her way back onto the porch. "You get outta here. Reggie ain't done nothing wrong, and I won't have you standing here telling me 'bout him. You don't know nothing 'bout us." Stella raised a shotgun and motioned with it for me to move back. Despite the situation, I could hear the banjo music in my head.

I raised my hands and stepped back, navigating the stairs with one hand on the railing. "If he's in trouble, Stella, maybe we can understand what happened. Why do you think he left town? Why didn't he tell you about his child?"

Stella shook her head and raised the shotgun. "This is private property, and I'm telling you to leave. You have no business here."

"Yes, okay," I said. "I'm going. Just think about it, Stella. Reggie might not be the man you think he is. If he's in trouble, what happens to you? You left your job, and they're unlikely to take you back. How will you support yourself?"

Stella kept the shotgun raised, but her hands shook. She might shoot me if I became aggressive, but she didn't look like someone who would fire at someone's back. But what did I know about her? Or Reggie, for that matter.

At the bottom of the stairs, I turned around and strode toward the car, my breath heavy and my heart racing. As soon as I was in the car, Christie took off down the long, winding road. I'd never been so thankful to leave a place in all my life, and considering Christie's fingers gripping the steering wheel and her colour-drained face, she felt the same.

Chapter 37

Later that afternoon, when my nerves had calmed, I wandered into the kitchen for a cup of coffee, considering what I might do next. Christie followed, still shaken from our encounter with Stella, while Hugo bounded toward me, eager for pats.

To my surprise, James was sitting with my mother at the kitchen island. They both turned as we entered the room.

"Oh, there you are. I was getting worried," Mom said. Her shoulders relaxed, but her facial features remained tight.

I glanced at Christie, who shrugged. Neither of us had told her where we were going. "What's going on?"

"Elsi's been theorizing that you and Christie went to confront someone about the murders without telling the police—or us—what the plan was. Is that about right?" I'd never heard James scold before, but he was clearly on my mother's side on this one.

I poured coffee for Christie, who took a seat beside my mother, and another for myself. How to explain myself?

"What gave you that idea?" Curious now about how she always knew everyone's business.

"Well, I had a hunch. You rarely take your car anywhere unless it's far. And you left Hugo with me," she said, nodding to the sunspot Hugo had found to lie in by the breakfast nook door. "And I noticed Christie called earlier—the ringtone, you know." She was right. I had different ringtones for everyone. Christie's was Carole King's "You've Got a Friend." "You didn't tell me where you were going, and that's very unusual."

"Okay, Miss Marple. So you just assumed I was confronting a suspect?"

"Yes," James and Mom said in unison.

I plopped myself into a chair and nodded. "You got me. But we weren't actually confronting a suspect, but a suspect's girlfriend."

"Go on," James said. I could tell he was a little hurt that we hadn't invited him to the party, but I didn't want to bring along someone who might intimidate the woman either. I had a better chance of swaying her if I spoke to her honestly.

"Reggie White's partner, Stella, was at Old Jackson's—I mean, his place—but Reggie wasn't home. I asked Stella if she was aware of Eloise. She clearly wasn't. In fact, I think she was upset about the whole thing. She also said Reggie hadn't been in town for days. That's suspicious, don't you think?"

"You're leaving something out," Christie said, crossing her arms.

I glared at her. Hadn't we agreed in the car to keep that detail to ourselves?

"Sorry, Minna." Christie explained how Stella had held me at gunpoint and how we had driven like mad away from the place.

My mother covered her mouth, her eyes wide. "She could have—"

"Mom, it's okay. Stella was upset, but she was more afraid than I was. She just wanted to scare me." I wasn't entirely sure I was right, but there was no reason to worry my mother any further.

"So your new theory is Reggie is Eloise's father, and he had some kind of disagreement with Richard Alcott, and then Norah?" James' eyebrows knitted together. He cupped his large hands around his coffee mug, elbows just off the table.

"I'm not sure of anything just yet, but Stella's behaviour sure confirms her worry about what he's done. If he hadn't told her about Eloise, that might have been enough for her, but I suspect there's something else going on there. If nothing else, he might be Eloise's father."

"The photo Eloise took could have been of Reggie and Stella," Christie said. "They are about the right size."

"I thought of that, too. Richard died of poisoning. They could have poisoned him and then driven him to the house. It would have been easier for two people to drag him."

"You found two glasses of whiskey on the kitchen table. One was empty. Maybe Reggie or Stella put poison in it," Christie suggested.

"Or one of them held the napkin over his mouth until he inhaled the poison and asphyxiated." I said. "But how did they even get one of those napkins? They weren't guests." There were too many options. We might have this all wrong.

I glanced at James, who took out his phone and was texting. "What are you doing?"

"I've just got an idea. My dad sees Reggie at the hardware store. He's always trying to fix leaks and other problems at that shack. I've asked him to let me know the next time he hears from Reggie. When he's back in town, he's likely to stop by."

"Good idea," I said. "In the meantime, I want to make a plan. We need to talk to Reggie in person. It's the only way we'll find out what really happened."

"Oh no, you don't!" My mother hit the table with her palm. "You're not going out there again. Not with some crazy armed woman waiting for you."

I sighed and nodded. "Stella didn't want to hurt me, but I hear you. This time, we'll make a solid plan that will keep everyone safe, and I promise I won't go anywhere without telling you."

"Fine, but I don't like it one bit." Mom stood up and wrapped her arms around my shoulders. "If there is one thing I've learned, it's that if you get something in your mind, nothing can stop you. Just be safe, kulta."

"I will," I said, feeling the warmth of her hug. It was wise of me to remember I had my mom and daughter to think about, too.

Chapter 38

James and I stood in the empty attic. The window was open, letting in fresh air, and James had finished vacuuming up the debris with his shop vac. Hugo sat on the top step watching our every movement, probably wondering why we'd been spending so much time up here lately.

"It looks a lot bigger without the furniture," I said. "Wonder what old Fanny thinks about it."

"I'm guessing she wished her husband had finished this part of the house. Attics really collect a lot of stuff over the decades." Just then, his phone pinged. He glanced at the screen. "It's Dad. Reggie came by to pick up some two-by-fours he'd ordered. Looks like he's back in town."

"This is it," I said, my heart fluttering with excitement, but my stomach knotting in dread. "I'm texting Christie now." By the time we got there, maybe Reggie would have fixed his broken porch step.

We dropped everything and headed down the back stairs into the kitchen, and through the breakfast nook towards James's truck.

"Just a second," I said, turning toward the garden. My mom was kneeling down by her tomato plants, her hat covering her face. "Mom, this is it. Can you take care of Hugo?"

Mom stood up, a look of dismay crossing her face. "Yes, of course. Be careful out there. I have my cellphone with me. Keep me posted."

"Of course. We'll be back in no time," I said. It was hard to sound reassuring when I wasn't so sure about our plan, but there was no turning back now. Well, that's not true. We could turn back any time we wanted to, but I didn't want to. I wanted this whole mess sorted out, and soon. How could Hygge House survive another murder?

James started the truck, and we zoomed toward Christie's place, a few blocks from Heritage Street in a neighbourhood of heritage homes. It was a lovely house, slightly on the smaller side, but suited her perfectly. A century earlier, it had been a speakeasy owned by a bootlegger. She loved its history.

As we pulled up beside the house, I saw her sitting on her front steps, her cellphone gripped in her hand.

"You ready for this?" I asked.

Christie nodded. "I have my orders, and I'm ready to execute them."

In James's truck, the long drive to Reggie's place seemed less bumpy, but just as long as the first time. Reggie's old Ford was in front of the house, so James found a place to turn around so we wouldn't get stuck behind him.

"You sure about this?" James asked, glancing from me to Christie. We both nodded.

Christie got out her cellphone and started filming, zooming in so that she could capture everything, while I made sure the microphone I'd attached to myself was on.

James strode beside me. If Reggie was here, he would think twice about messing with James, but it irked me he wouldn't feel as intimidated by me.

I skipped the broken stair and knocked loudly. "Stella, it's me. Can we talk?"

Stella came straight to the door, her eyes wild and hair dishevelled. "Don't you know nothing? Go away. Reggie's not here." Her voice was a dramatic whisper, but her eyes were a little wild, even fearful.

"Isn't that his truck?" James asked, motioning toward the driveway.

Stella's face reddened. "He's not here, I mean. At the house. He's out ..."

I raised my eyebrows. "Are you sure about that? If Reggie is innocent, why wouldn't he want to talk to us? We're not the police. We don't have any weapons." I held up my hands as if to prove I wasn't carrying anything.

Stella made the slightest movement to look behind her, or maybe to grab the shotgun kept beside the door, but James was faster than she was. He easily grabbed it out of her hands and removed the shells. "Easy does it, Stella. We're not here to hurt anyone. Do you mind if I take a quick look?"

Stella crumpled onto the porch, not even attempting to stop him. We heard a scuffle and some yelling.

I ran around to the back of the shack. Reggie White flung open the back door and was sprinting across the yard toward the woods. I sprinted after him. My lungs burned in no time, but I wasn't about to let Reggie disappear into the forest. Within a few feet, I had tackled him, and we were on the ground, him trying to release my hold; me trying to hold on for dear life.

The next moment, I heard a loud voice yell out. "Freeze!"

I stopped, raising both hands and turning slowly. Officer Grey held out her weapon, pointed at Reggie. "On your knees," she said. Reggie did as he commanded, and I moved a safe distance away.

The plan had worked. Christie had called the police before we left her place and confirmed as soon as she saw Reggie's truck. James confronted him, and I was ready if he ran. The only thing now was to confirm Reggie was who we thought he was.

Chapter 39

I sat on the ground and caught my breath while Officer Grey cuffed Reggie. James reached his hand out, and I took it, rising from the ground.

Reggie scowled at me. "You meddling people," he said. "Why didn't you leave it alone?"

"Why did you do it, Reggie? Something happened when you were kids, and Richard Alcott knew all about it. So did Norah. Richard was so worried about coming back to town, he was going to skip his favourite nephew's wedding."

Officer Grey guided Reggie toward the house, and we walked at a slow pace.

"Why do you think? Rickie was going to rat me out. Everyone would know what had happened, and I would end up in jail."

I glanced at James. This was the missing piece. "What was Richard going to tell?"

Reggie stifled a sob. "I didn't mean to kill that girl." It surprised me to see him upset.

"You mean Norah?"

"The tourist girl. Rickie, Norah, and me went to a beach party, just west of Driftwood Cottages. They were by the bonfire, talking about stuff and ignoring me. I knew Rickie had a thing for Norah. I was upset with both of them, so I wandered off. Met a pretty girl—a tourist—and we got to talking for a while."

Reggie hung his head, tears flowing down his face now.

"What happened to the girl, Reggie?"

"We went for a swim and things got a little heated, if you know what I mean. I'd had too much to drink. We went into the water, fooling around. And then ... she just disappeared."

"What do you mean?" I hadn't expected yet another body. Nothing had prepared me for this story.

Reggie looked at me with tears in his eyes. "I looked for her. I got Norah and Rickie to search, too, but she was gone. It was too dark. We couldn't see anything in the water. I didn't mean to ..."

"Why didn't you go to the police?"

Reggie hung his head. "I was scared. The police had already picked me for some minor stuff. Thought I was a trouble-maker. What if they thought I killed that girl? I couldn't chance it. Rickie wanted to go to the police, but I made them both promise never to tell."

"So Richard was going to come clean about what happened that night and implicate you. His conscience was too heavy to keep it a secret any longer."

"I went to Crow's Nest to talk to him about it, but he said he had to tell the police. Said he'd been keeping too many secrets and couldn't do it anymore. Wanted to come clean to his lady, Lillian. He wanted me to come with him, but I couldn't let that happen. My record's not exactly clean, you know."

"So you enlisted Stella to drive your truck to Hygge House? You poisoned Rickie and dragged him to the Muskoka chair, leaving him there to be found later. How did you get the pink napkin?"

Reggie looked confused. "Stella noticed that the catering van door was open. She grabbed one."

Huh. I hadn't thought about Michael's van. He stocked everything he needed. "Stella used the rake to cover the tracks. You left his car and took your truck. And she wrote the notes, didn't she?" I remembered the calligraphy pen and her tidy writing in the guest book at Driftwood Cottages.

Reggie nodded. "Stella didn't want to be involved, but we had no choice ..."

James shook his head. "Man, you always have a choice. But why Norah?"

"Norah told me Rickie had had a conversation with her and was going to the police right after the wedding. When Rickie ... died ... Norah said she would report it herself. We were playing at the rich guy's cottage party. I fixed her drink and gave it to her as a peace offering. She got sick, and Zander drove her home. Dead by morning."

"Did you know Norah had a child? Eloise?" I asked, watching for his reaction. Now, we were approaching the front of the house where the police vehicles were waiting, and Detective Whitford was jotting in his notebook as he talked to Christie.

"Yeah, I knew. But it's not mine. I swear. Zander and Norah were on and off again over the years. She got pregnant but couldn't raise the child. She never told him, but she told me."

"Why would she tell you?" I asked, curious about the timeline.

"Don't know. We were at Evan Lahti's cottage party, and Norah said she'd met her daughter, Eloise, and she couldn't live with herself if she let another secret stay buried. She told me not to worry; it wasn't mine and then admitted it was Zander's. She planned on telling him everything."

"But she never got the chance." I crossed my arms and stared into Reggie's eyes. "And the poison?"

"Strychnine. I keep it in the glove compartment. It wasn't how I wanted things to go. Believe me," Reggie said.

"But you can't even buy strychnine anymore. It's illegal," James said.

"Sure, but I worked out west at a national park in Alberta. We used it out there quite a bit, mostly for gopher control. Brought some back with me. Kept it in the shed, but I had some in the glove compartment, too. Used it a few times over the years—wolves on the property. Never thought I'd need to use it on a person." Reggie stifled a sob as if the memory was too painful to bear. "And Stella. She's not at fault for anything."

I turned to where Stella was being cuffed by a police officer before entering the police car. "I guess that's up to the police," I said, glancing at Detective Whitford.

Whitford nodded solemnly, and Officer Grey brought Reggie into her police cruiser.

"Well, Minna. I'd say I am impressed, but that might give you ideas. I'll need you to come to the station and fill in all the details." Whitford paused. "Good work. Just don't do it again."

"Of course not," I said. "We don't intend to have any more murders at Hygge House, or in Lakewood for that matter."

Chapter 40

M id-morning sun shone through the windows of the sunroom, dancing across the table, laid with dinnerware and cutlery, with a buffet of breakfast foods on the side table. Vases filled with flowers from Mom's garden provided bright colour against the light tones of the interior walls and flooring.

I sipped my coffee and surveyed the room, filled with my loved ones and friends—new and old—and held back tears. Sometimes, on days like today, it was like living a fairy tale. A castle-like house with friends coming and going, a magical garden with fairy sprites, a shining lake, and a mysterious forest. And best of all, a happy ending. What more could one ask for?

"Everything all right, Mom?" Sofia asked as she added blueberry jam to a croissant.

"Better than alright," I said, beaming at my daughter. "I just feel so much ... joy. I can't even describe it."

Sofia smiled but appeared puzzled. "You must be relieved it's all over. Now you can relax."

From my vantage point at the head of the table, I had the perfect view of the families gathered here. Jack and Grace sat with Lillian, her bags already packed and sitting on the verandah, ready for her departure after this one last meal together. They chatted about the recent events, but also about the young couple's plans to buy a house in Lakewood, and Lillian's promise to visit often.

Tyler sat beside Sofia, and watching their relaxed chatter and laughter lightened my heart. Sofia had planned to stay in

Lakewood until the end of the summer, but she might have a reason to stay longer. I hoped so.

James sat at the other end of the table, catching my eye throughout breakfast, with his father Henri to his left and my mother to his right. James raised his eyebrows when my mother and his father seemed deep in conversation. I couldn't catch what they were saying, but clearly James felt like the third wheel. Sofia might be right about a romance between our parents. Time would tell.

Floyd sat beside Christie, enjoying Finnish pancakes and an assortment of fruit. It was nice to see her dating app on hold, at least for the moment.

She stood up and clinked her crystal water glass. "I just want to take a few moments to say thank you for coming this morning. It was a last-minute invitation, but Minna and I wanted a final gathering before Lillian's departure. We've had a rough start to Hygge House, but with your kindness and support, we're looking forward to brighter days ahead."

The guests nodded, and murmurs of assent filled the space.

Christie turned to me. "And to our very own Nancy Drew, thank you. Lakewood is better because of you."

"Hear, hear," James called out from the end of the table, grinning as he winked at me. He stood up, producing a bouquet wrapped in pretty white paper and a pale yellow ribbon I'd seen at Winterberry and Willow. He crossed the room and handed them to me, and if I were a swooner, I would have swooned.

"To Minna," Christie said, and everyone chimed in. "To Minna."

Heat rose in my cheeks, and I had no words to express my thoughts, but Christie encouraged me to stand up and speak. I held the bouquet in my arms as if I'd just won Miss America or something. All I needed was the crown. Luckily, the only one in the room who had a crown was Grace.

"I don't know what to say, but my heart is full looking at all of you gathered around this table. I'm happy I could help Jack and Grace, and of course, Lillian." The newlyweds exchanged glances, looking happier and more at peace than I'd seen them in months. Lillian dabbed her eyes and smiled, mouthing 'thank you' to me. "And of course, Floyd. You've lost friends and bandmates, but you always told the truth to help us solve this mystery. Christie and I thank you all for your love and support. It's because of all of you that Hygge House is still standing."

Floyd nodded solemnly and thanked me. I sat back down and finished my breakfast, pouring myself another cup of coffee as the conversation flowed freely around the table.

As breakfast wound down, our guests stood up and mingled, saying goodbye to each other. Lillian approached and enclosed me in a long hug. "He was the love of my life. I loved Jack's father, but Richard was my soul-mate. You have given me so much peace. And you have made Hygge House a second home. I look forward to returning soon. And I hope I can have Fanny's room. She and I have become quite close." Lillian winked and smiled at my mother, and I didn't know what to say.

Jack stood beside his mother, his hand in Grace's, clearly emotional from his mother's words. "I was so angry that Uncle Rick wasn't coming to the wedding, but now I understand why. He wanted to do the right thing, to be the person I knew he was, and to come clean to the police about what had happened all those years ago. Knowing he planned on attending the wedding, despite his worries about returning to Lakewood, well, it means the world to me."

Grace nodded and gave me a hug. She whispered in my ear, and my eyes widened, but I promised not to reveal her secret just yet. She beamed at me as she pulled away, a twinkle in her eyes. A new life was the hope for the future, and she deserved all the blessings she would receive. Her fairy-tale wedding may have ended in disaster, but she had years of happiness ahead of her, with a little prince or princess on the way.

After our guests departed, Christie and I sat on the porch swing together, our feet pushing it in unison as if we were twelve years old again. I linked my arm through hers.

"Hygge House will survive all this, won't it?" I asked. I'd tried not to think too much about the effect of this second murder on our business venture, but the reality had come crashing in again now that the police had arrested and charged Reggie and Stella.

"Are you kidding?" Christie said. We're booked for the entire summer and already getting bookings for the fall. That reminds me, the Fall Fair is such a big event that we need to get going on our plans soon." Christie stood up and grabbed her oversized bag, pulling out her clipboard. "I have a few ideas I want to run by you."

"I bet you do," I said, leaning over her shoulder. Christie had a long list of events already created, and she ran through them quickly. I might be creative in design, but Christie knew how to bring people in.

"Mom mentioned that the organizing committee for the Fall Fair has already met. They've nominated her as the chair. She's thrilled," I said. "It also means we'll all have jobs to do, I bet."

Christie laughed. "What about Hygge House? What's next on the renovation plans?"

"Now that we've planned the attic space, James is going to work on it over the summer. We'll have it ready in September. But I have a few other ideas to float by you—"

Just then, my phone pinged. "It's a text from Eloise," I said. "She wants to reserve a room with us for all of August. She's moving back to Lakewood so she can get to know her father—Zander."

"Zander?" Christie said. "How did she find out he was her dad?"

I shrugged. "Norah must have told her the truth before she flew to Paris. Or maybe Zander reached out to her. Looks like selfie-girl wants to spend time with us until she finds a place to live."

Christie laughed. "At least she'll bring us some good publicity," she said, and I agreed.

We resumed our swinging, and I leaned my head against Christie's shoulder, breathing in the scent of lilacs. The summer was truly upon us now, and I wanted to capture the feeling we'd had as kids—long summer days and free spirits—ready to take on the world and create our own adventures. My fairy-tale life was here, with my friends and family, in this grand old lady of a house where every day was a magical surprise.

Acknowledgements

Writing book two of the series was just as much fun as writing the first one, and I hope readers will enjoy it, too. Thank you to Kim Reynolds for working with me through the planning process. Your insights are always so valuable. And big thanks to Jill G. Durkin for her excellent editing.

Sending thanks and gratitude to my Women Writing Circle, who show up to support one another in reaching their writing goals. You continue to inspire me. To my writing group—Holly, Emily, Shanon, Lindsay, and Greg—thank you for your friendship. To the members of the Sudbury Writers' Guild, your support continues to encourage me. Many thanks to Sisters in Crime, Toronto Chapter, for welcoming me into the sisterhood.

Continued love and gratitude to my circle of support, especially my mom, Anja. And to Francine, Tom and Carita, Judith and Scott, Kristin and Hideki, Megan, Russell and Jeanna, and my nieces and nephews, as well as my new great-nephews, Boaz and Arthur, much love. Finally, to Michael, Mia, and Kieran, there are no words to share how much you mean to me.

About the Author

A. L. Jensen is a Finnish-Canadian author and certified book coach. An empty nester, she lives with her husband, Michael, on a serene lake in the small community of Naughton in Greater Sudbury, Ontario. When she's not writing and sipping chai lattes at her local coffee shop, you'll find her reading in her gazebo, or walking nearby trails with her Mini Goldendoodle, Emmy, while dreaming of her next travel adventure. As Liisa Kovala, she is also the award-winning author of *Like Water For Weary Souls* (House of Karhu, 2025), *Sisu's Winter War* (Latitude 46, 2022), and *Surviving Stutthof* (Latitude 46, 2017). Learn more at aljensenauthor.com and subscribe to liisakovalawomenwriting.substack.com.

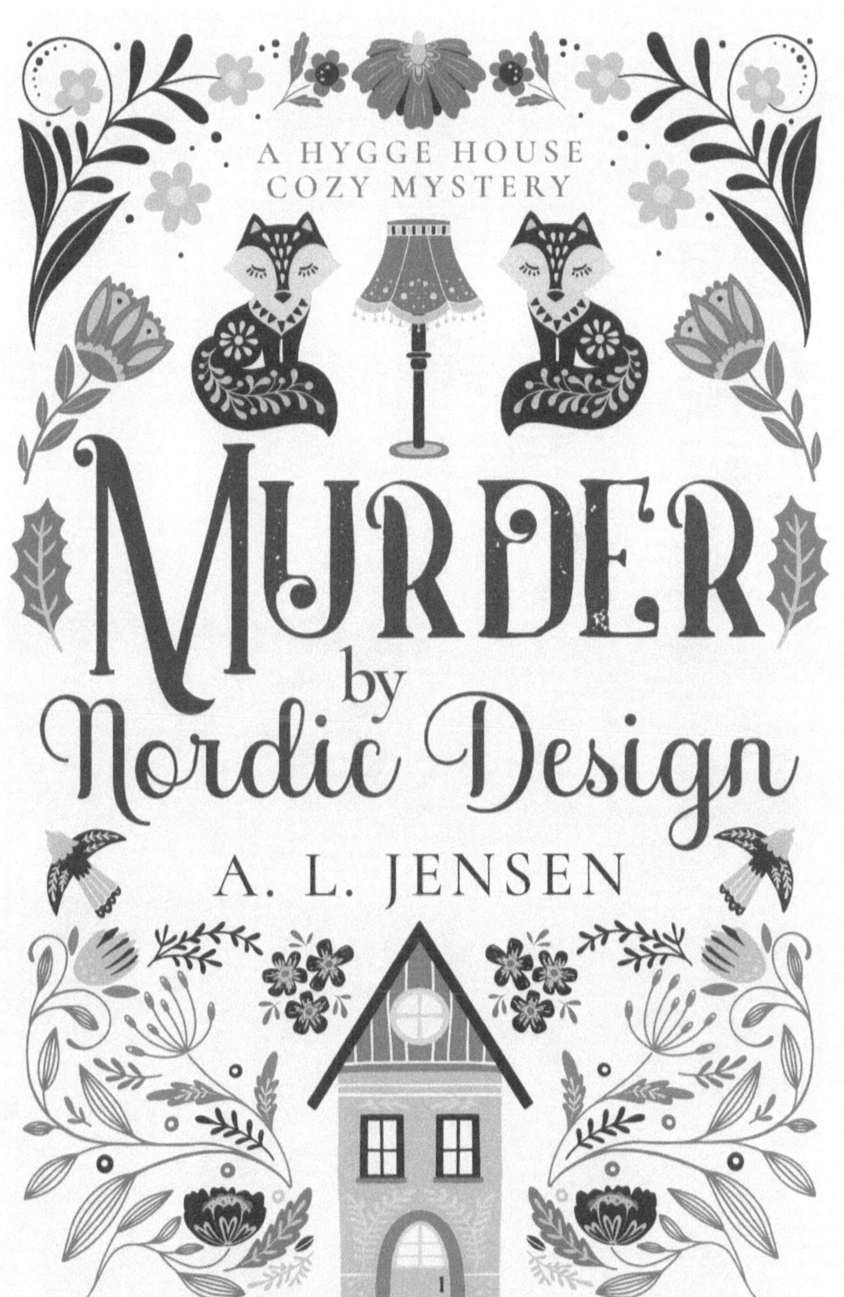

A HYGGE HOUSE
COZY MYSTERY
MURDER
by
Nordic Design
A. L. JENSEN

The cool water skimmed my body as I pulled forward, legs fluttering and arms reaching. Halfway across the lake, I paused, trying to catch my breath, eggbeater kicks keeping me afloat. Mist rose softly around me, and I could barely make out the form of Hygge House across the smooth lake. The place was quiet at this time in the morning, before James and his carpentry crew arrived to create a cacophony of noise as they worked on the sauna and finished the last cottage.

Despite the serenity of this moment, I had a lot to do. With Lakewood's Fall Fair only weeks away, Christie and I had plans, and my mother, Elsi—organizing this year's event—had plans for us, too. With long, steady strokes, I swam back to our new dock where Hugo Dogberg waited. He could barely contain himself as I approached, his tail swinging wildly.

"It's okay, boy. I'm almost there," I said in a reassuring voice in response to Hugo's spontaneous barks. Was he worried about my safety? I mean, swimming alone might not be the safest option, but James's carpentry crew would be here at any minute. Another reason to get out of the lake. There was nothing like hammers and saws to interrupt one's peace.

At the dock, I pulled myself up the ladder and plopped beside Hugo, wrapping a large towel around my shoulders. Compared to the lake, the morning air was chilly. I shivered. Hugo Dogberg lapped the water from my foot, happier now that I was safely on shore.

Every morning since summer began, I'd taken advantage of the warmer days to get in a morning swim, and despite September's cooler temperatures, I was determined to keep up the habit. Since moving to Lakewood earlier in the year, my fitter body had given me more energy. Regular swims and walks in the woods, plus using my bike, Tuuli, as my primary transportation, had done this old body good. I glanced behind me at the partially built sauna. Once it was complete, I'd be able to swim all year around. Nothing was better for physical and mental health than a sauna.

Hugo turned and barked, bounding away. I gathered my things, wrapped my towel around my body, and slipped into flip-flops.

"How was the water this morning?" James asked, tool belt slung across his hips and two coffee cups from Boreal Beanery in his hands. He handed one to me. I accepted gratefully.

"Water's fine. It's the air that's chilly now. Can't beat the view, though." I gestured across the lake, mist rising from the surface, creating a surreal panorama. "What's on the agenda for today?"

James took a sip of coffee. "Foundation's done, so we'll work on getting the walls up. I'm putting Abby and Lucas on the last mökki. It should be ready in a day or two."

"Great. I can't wait to get my hands on that last cottage. Christie's already booked the three mökkis for the entire week of the Fall Fair. I want them to be perfect." I appreciated the warmth emanating from the coffee cup, but still shivered. "There's a lot to do. Do you think we'll be ready?" I didn't want to pressure James any more than he already felt, but I couldn't help but feel anxious about the timelines.

He rubbed his stubbled chin and nodded. "There's still time, and I'll get it done if I have to work day and night. I promise."

"I hope you don't have to do that. At least you have a good crew working with you." There was no way James could have accomplished a new dock, three one-bedroom cottages and a sauna all by himself this summer. He was a workhorse, but these projects required several skilled carpenters.

He sighed and took another sip of coffee. "Yeah, they're good at their jobs, that's for sure."

"How's Tim working out?" I'd convinced James to hire Brian Bean's younger cousin for the summer, but I knew he could be a handful.

"Tim? Yeah, he's a good kid, overall. If he'd get to work on time." I could tell he was holding back. It wasn't the first time he had complained about his crew. Lukas, Abby, Matti and Jen knew their jobs, but didn't always get along. "Hang in there, James. The projects are nearly done."

James nodded and smiled. "I don't mean to complain. They're all excellent. You can't expect people to get along all the time. I just wish I knew what the problems are so I can help."

Just like James to want to solve the problem. "I don't think you can help them with their differences. Not if they don't want it. Besides, they're all adults. They'll sort it out."

"That's what I'm afraid of."

Just then, the four carpenters strode towards the sauna. Abby smiled and waved toward us, and I waved back. She seemed like a pleasant, easy-going girl. Jen was speaking non-stop to Matti, her arms gesturing wildly, but Matti only nodded politely and barely responded. And Lukas dropped his stuff off, a scowl on his face I recognized too well. A

"You have your work cut out for you," I said. "Let me know if you need anything today. I'll be working from the house with Christie." I called Hugo, who had sprinted to Matti for pats. Hugo ran back to me, giving Lukas a wide berth. Even Hugo knew Lukas was in a perpetually bad mood. "Oh, and Sofia mentioned she wants to take some photos for the social media account."

James agreed. "Before and afters are a great idea. I'll make sure the crew is on their best behaviour."

I laughed. "Good luck with that." I turned toward the house. The swim had lifted my spirits. And James's reassurance always gave me confidence. Besides, nothing untoward had happened at Hygge House since Grace and Jack's wedding in June. We'd had a busy and productive summer. Things were definitely on the upswing. A few minutes later, Tim was jogging across the lawn. Late again.

I envisioned our finished sauna and the atmosphere I wanted to create for its christening during the Fall Fair. The heat from the stove, the sizzle from the steam, soft light from candles on the dock. Hygge House could become the ultimate destination for health and wellness, and I knew our guests would love it. I hugged myself in delight and bounded up the stairs to my room for a shower. Christie would be here soon, and we had plans to arrange and checklists to check. We were finally making Hygge House the destination we'd dreamed of creating, and nothing was going to stand in our way.

Murder by Nordic Design, Book 3 in the Hygge House Cozy Mystery series, available on August 3, 2026. Pre-order now.

www.ingramcontent.com/pod-product-compliance
Lightning Source LLC
Chambersburg PA
CBHW032011050726
47590CB00006B/2131